Embroidery Cottage

De-ann Black

Paperback edition published 2022

Embroidery Cottage

ISBN: 9798443028026

Also by De-ann Black (Romance, Action/Thrillers & Children's books). See her Amazon Author page or website for further details about her books, screenplays, illustrations, art and fabric designs.
www.De-annBlack.com

Romance:

The Dressmaker's Cottage
The Sewing Shop
Heather Park
The Tea Shop by the Sea
The Bookshop by the Seaside
The Sewing Bee
The Quilting Bee
Snow Bells Wedding
Snow Bells Christmas
Summer Sewing Bee
The Chocolatier's Cottage
Christmas Cake Chateau
The Beemaster's Cottage
The Sewing Bee By The Sea
The Flower Hunter's Cottage

The Christmas Knitting Bee
The Sewing Bee & Afternoon Tea
The Vintage Sewing & Knitting Bee
Shed In The City
The Bakery By The Seaside
Champagne Chic Lemonade Money
The Christmas Chocolatier
The Christmas Tea Shop & Bakery
The Vintage Tea Dress Shop In Summer
Oops! I'm The Paparazzi
The Bitch-Proof Suit

Action/Thrillers:

Love Him Forever.
Someone Worse.
Electric Shadows.

The Strife Of Riley.
Shadows Of Murder.

Colouring books:

Summer Garden. Spring Garden. Autumn Garden. Sea Dream.
Festive Christmas. Christmas Garden. Flower Bee. Wild Garden.
Faerie Garden Spring. Flower Hunter. Stargazer Space. Bee Garden.

Embroidery books:

Floral Garden Embroidery Patterns
Floral Spring Embroidery Patterns
Christmas & Winter Embroidery Patterns
Floral Nature Embroidery Designs
Scottish Garden Embroidery Designs

Contents

Chapter One   1
Chapter Two   9
Chapter Three   18
Chapter Four   30
Chapter Five   39
Chapter Six   48
Chapter Seven   58
Chapter Eight   68
Chapter Nine   77
Chapter Ten   87

Embroidery Pattern Downloads   102

About De-ann Black   107

CHAPTER ONE

Euan hurried across one of his flower fields, taking a shortcut through the fragrant blooms, heading straight for Minnie's grocery shop by the sea.

Several small shops including a tea shop, dress shop and a bar restaurant were dotted along the esplanade down by the little harbour. The early morning blinked awake against the sunlight glinting off the surface of the calm sea. White clouds across the bay's coastline hadn't yet burned off to reveal a clear blue sky. The fresh sea air had an added hint of autumn to it as the last lingering warmth of the long, hot summer gave way to the next season. Euan's favourite season. He loved the spring and summer for the wonderful array of flowers that he grew, but there was something about the autumn that filled his senses with excitement. The rich, vibrant tones of the autumn flowers — the burgundy, burnt orange and deep golden yellow, suited his character and were a fair match for his dress sense. The muted green corduroy trousers, sturdy ochre boots and classic moss green jacket blended with the Scottish seaside scenery. Euan would've blended better if he hadn't been so tall and strikingly handsome. The flurry of burnished gold hair and handsome face made Euan stand out from the scenery while appearing entirely at home in his farmhouse and flower fields setting.

The phone call from a potential client — a woman responding to his advertisement, set his hopes alight. He'd recently bought a neighbouring field from a farmer wishing to retire. The field was separated by a narrow road from his main field, but the close proximity made it handy for cultivation. A field whose rich soil was perfect for new flower growing. But the field came with a cottage as part of the sale. A cottage that the farmer had no need of as he lived in a sizeable farmhouse, so he'd rented it out these past several years as a holiday cottage. Quite a few cottages in the little village on the West Coast of Scotland were leased out to holidaymakers throughout the year especially during the height of summer and at Christmastime. Euan hadn't planned to acquire this property as he too had a substantial farmhouse and until he'd decided what to do with the spare cottage, he'd advertised it as a cottage for rent. The interior was spick and span, and it was kitted out with every comfort. He hadn't expected it to be snapped up so quickly, but the woman he'd just spoken to sounded ideal. She wanted to move in right away, eager to leave her flat in Glasgow and set up home along with a small craft business she planned to run from the cottage.

Euan would've agreed to the lease, a temporary one, until he was sure of her character, but she wanted to know about something that he had no idea about — embroidery. Specifically, was there enough daylight shining in through the living room windows to allow her to embroider in natural light? Unsure, he'd set off to ask Minnie for her opinion. Their cottages were of a similar build and both faced the sea, so he assumed she'd know if it was suitable, especially as Minnie was one of the main members of the local quilting bee. The ladies held their quilting bee nights in the function room at the back of Gordon's tea shop. He trusted that Minnie would know about embroidering in the cottage.

Euan hurried into Minnie's shop, a well-stocked grocery shop and the hub of the local gossiping community, trailing in a gust of sea air with him in his rush.

'Minnie!' Euan gasped, interrupting her chat to one of the customers — Pearl, another member of the quilting bee. Fit and fifties, with light auburn hair and rosy cheeks.

Minnie blinked. 'What's wrong, Euan? You look flustered.' In her fifties, she had a cheerful manner and wore her brown hair pinned up in a tidy bun.

Bracken, Minnie's floppy eared dog, was curled up cosy in his basket with the new quilt she'd stitched for him. She made a new one for him every season, and extras too if she had a notion to make one from her latest quilt fabric scraps. Bracken was popular with customers and had black, white and brown fur. At the sound of Euan's voice, the dog looked as alert as he was going to be that early in the day. His tail wagged a couple of times, and then he nodded off to sleep again.

'I need your advice,' Euan told her quickly. 'About embroidery.'

Minnie frowned and shared a questioning glance with Pearl. 'Embroidery?'

By now, another customer had walked in — Gordon, owner of the tea shop, eager to buy more strawberry jam for the Victoria

2

sponge cakes he was baking. Gordon, thirties, was of similar age and stature to Euan, with blue–green eyes and tawny hair, and had already gone for his daily dip in the sea that kept his build fit and strong.

'Finally giving in and joining the ladies quilting bee, Euan?' Gordon quipped, catching the tail end of the conversation.

Euan gave an exasperated sigh. 'No, you won't get me to sew anything more than a button on my shirts, and I'm certainly not planning to learn embroidery.'

'So what do you want to know?' Minnie asked Euan.

He summarised about his situation while everyone in the shop listened and contributed their opinion.

'I've just spoken to her on the phone,' Euan explained. 'I didn't know if there was enough natural light shining in through the cottage windows for her to stitch her embroidery without having to set up special lighting. I said I'd find out and call her right back. So if you could help me, I'd appreciate it.'

'I get plenty of daylight through my front windows,' said Minnie. 'My cottage and the one in your new field both face the sea, so she's bound to have as much daylight as me.'

Euan let go of the breath he was holding. 'Thank goodness. I was hoping you'd say that.' He took out his phone and was about to call her when he had an idea. 'I don't suppose you'd talk to her. She might ask another embroidery type question and I don't want to sound like a total fool.'

Minnie took charge of Euan's phone while Pearl and Gordon stood happily waiting to be served, and eager to hear the outcome of the call. She pressed the button to make the call and spoke to Euan while waiting on it being picked up. 'What's her name?'

'Poppy,' said Euan, secretly liking the sound of it, and the sound of the woman he'd just spoken to. Silly of him, he knew, but there was something in her tone, her manner, that clicked with him. 'It would be so handy if I could have the cottage rented out quickly. This is one of my busiest times of year — the end of summer and beginning of autumn. If this was settled it would be great.'

Euan was still talking when the call was picked up.

Minnie fumbled with the buttons, unfamiliar with Euan's phone, and accidentally put it on speaker.

'Hello, is that Poppy?' Minnie began.

'Yes,' an unsure voice replied.

'I'm a friend of Euan,' Minnie explained. 'He asked me to call you about the embroidery light issue with the cottage.'

The unsure voice changed to one of hopefulness. 'Yes, I'm really keen to take the cottage.'

It was only then that Euan realised he could hear every word that Poppy was saying. He glanced at Gordon and Pearl.

'Minnie's pressed the speakerphone button,' Gordon whispered to Euan.

Euan decided not to tell her, happy that he could hear what Poppy was saying...until the conversation became more of a woman to woman chat when Minnie revealed that she was a member of the quilting bee.

Not knowing that she could be overheard by Euan and the others, Poppy confided in Minnie, feeling an instant rapport with her due to their shared love of sewing.

'I didn't know there was a local quilting bee.' Poppy sounded enthusiastic.

'Yes, we have a quilting bee evening once a week at Gordon's tea shop down by the harbour,' Minnie told her. 'Twice a week if we have a quilting emergency.'

Poppy laughed. 'A quilting emergency?' She'd never heard of such a thing.

'We may be a small community, but we've a lot going on in the local area,' said Minnie. 'Quilting, sewing and all sorts of other crafts, like knitting and crochet, are part of our bee nights. Many of the members run small craft businesses from their homes, and we all muck in if there are extra orders of quilts or whatever is needed for customers. We all help each other.'

'It sounds wonderful. Such a strong community spirit,' said Poppy.

'Oh yes, and you'd be made very welcome,' Minnie told her. 'We have a few members who are keen embroiderers, and I enjoy a fair bit of embroidery myself. You'd fit right in with the bee.'

Poppy felt the excitement build inside her. The cottage sounded great, but to be part of a local quilting bee was a bonus she hadn't anticipated. 'I've never been to a sewing or quilting bee before, but I've always wanted to join something like that.'

'Well then, when you arrive, pop down to my grocery shop and I'll introduce you to some of the ladies.' Minnie was already talking as if the deal for the cottage had been sealed. Poppy made no attempt to reconsider taking on the lease. She liked the sound of the whole package — a traditional cottage by the sea, away from the hustle and bustle of the city, and invited to be part of the quilting bee. New friends, a new start.

'Euan's a fine young man,' said Minnie, 'and I'm sure you'll find him a great landlord, or whatever title he'll be.'

'He seemed keen to lease the cottage to me. There isn't anything I should know about him is there?' This was the first hint of hesitation in Poppy's voice.

'Oh, definitely not,' Minnie assured her. 'I've known Euan for years and he's a perfect gentleman. Too perfect if you ask me. That's why he's still single. A nice and successful man like him doesn't have much luck when it comes to the ladies. We've had a few young women here in the past months, wanting away from the city and a fresh start, but they've settled with someone else. Euan just isn't...lucky in love.'

'Huh! Tell me about it.' Poppy sighed heavily.

'You sound about the same age as Euan. He's in his early thirties,' said Minnie, hoping to find out more about Poppy.

'Yes, you're right. I'm thirty–one. I was involved with someone. My boss at the management firm I worked for in Glasgow, but I found out he was an untrustworthy rat and we broke up several months ago.'

'Oh, dear,' Minnie sympathised. 'I'm sorry you've been through the mill when it comes to men. Is that why you want to move here? A fresh start?'

'It is. I quit my job recently and I want to build up my embroidery business. I'd been working on it in the evenings. My ex told me I was wasting my time.'

'I think you're well rid of him,' said Minnie. 'And now you can concentrate on your craft business.'

'Exactly. I can work from anywhere, so I thought I'd get away from the city. The cottage by the sea sounds so tranquil.'

Minnie laughed. 'Be warned. We may have a lovely setting by the sea, but we're a busy wee community. Tranquil isn't quite what you'll find here. But we do offer a supportive community.'

5

'That sounds wonderful,' said Poppy. 'I guess...I really need to get over feeling heartbroken. I am over him, but it takes a lot out of you. Do you know what I mean? Sometimes I feel lost and then I have bags of enthusiasm and want to make lots of plans, then all it takes is for someone to say — you'll never make a proper living out of designing embroidery patterns and showing your stitching online.'

'The world is full of gloom merchants. Pay no heed whatsoever. Once you're with us, you'll have a chance to build up your wee business without having the emotional stuffing knocked out of you.'

'I'm going to take the cottage,' Poppy said firmly. 'Euan sounds trustworthy.'

'And he's handsome,' Minnie added.

Poppy giggled. 'Handsome?'

'Oh yes, he's a looker.'

Euan started to wave at Minnie, trying to get her to hush, but she continued and wouldn't let him grab the phone. She hurried behind the shop counter and pointed to the sign. No customers allowed behind the counter.

Euan stopped short and sighed with exasperation, while Gordon stifled his laughter.

Pearl enjoyed the gossip and was eager to hear how the conversation would unfold.

'Euan owns a lovely farmhouse, and his flower fields are beautiful,' Minnie elaborated. 'He makes a lot of money from his flowers, but he's already rich. Inherited wealth. Not that money is the enticement. But it just means that he's settled, with no financial worries. A bonus in itself.'

Poppy forgot for a moment that she wasn't talking to a long time friend and blurted out a comment that made Euan blush. 'Well, if Euan is as perfect and single and handsome as you say, maybe one day he will be lucky in love.'

The two women giggled, a moment of shared light–heartedness.

'He's got a nice voice,' Poppy remarked.

'A sexy voice,' Minnie blurted out. And then they giggled again.

Before Minnie had completely sold him as a potential boyfriend to Poppy, Euan reached over the counter and grabbed the phone. Fumbling for it, the call was disconnected.

Euan, now in charge of his phone, shook his head in dismay at Minnie. 'I just wanted you to assure her about the light in the cottage, not marry me off.'

'Och, it was just girl talk,' Minnie said, brushing his concerns aside. 'I'm sure she won't be the woman for you. There are plenty of eligible young men that she can have fun with. She sounds like she needs to have fun after the bitter relationship with her ex. Some men trample your dreams into the floorboards. I think she's better off without his sort, and she'll fit right into our bee nights.'

'I hope she'll share some of her embroidery patterns,' Pearl said to Minnie.

'She sounds the type that will want to join in and be part of our bee, so I'm sure we can all share our sewing and embroidery,' said Minnie.

Euan called Poppy. He pressed his finger to his lips and glanced at Minnie, Pearl and Gordon to indicate that he didn't want her to know that the previous conversation hadn't been private.

'Poppy? Did Minnie explain and assure you about the cottage?' said Euan.

'Yes, I'll take the lease. And I didn't know that there was a quilting bee. So that's sealed the deal for me.'

'Great. I'll email the details and you can let me know when you want to arrive.'

'Would later today be too soon?'

'Eh, no, the cottage is clean and tidy. You can arrive as soon as you want. What about the place you're living in now, in the city?'

'The lease is due to end soon and that's why I'd already been looking for somewhere else to stay when I saw the advert for the cottage. I share a flat in Glasgow with a colleague and she's planning to move in with her boyfriend. So I've got my belongings packed. Not that I own a lot. It's a furnished rental, so I've only got my clothes and my embroidery work. It would all fit into my car.'

During the past couple of weeks she'd been systematically discarding clothes and other items she'd outworn or didn't use, and this had drastically cut down on her packing. She hadn't dreamed that she'd move into a seaside cottage, and anticipated another lease in a Glasgow flat. City rents were quite expensive and it worked out that the cottage was marginally less per month. A definite win–win situation. An affordable cottage and a wonderful sea and countryside

7

location. With no relatives left since her elderly aunt and uncle passed, and without the anchor of a job weighing her down, she was free to take off on this exciting adventure.

She queried about the directions to the cottage.

'Once you're on the main route out of the city, head for the coast road,' Euan explained. 'I'll email directions from there. We're quite tricky to find at first, nestled into the countryside. You won't be able to see the cottage for the trees until you drive further down the road. It'll all be on the map, and if you get lost call me and I'll drive up and find you.'

'I'll see you later then, Euan.'

'Yes, see you later.' Euan ended the call and seemed a little bit fazed.

'That went well,' Gordon remarked. 'She might be here in time for tonight's quilting bee. Do you think I should ice her name on one of my cakes as a welcoming?'

'Yes, do that,' said Minnie. 'If she's not here in time, we'll scoff it anyway.'

Euan felt as if the situation was drifting out of his control but tried to sound confident. 'I guess I'll make sure the cottage is stocked with fresh groceries for Poppy.'

'Fresh milk, butter, cheese, bread and other bits and bobs is all you need,' Minnie told him. 'Once she's settled in, she can select what she likes.'

'I've cleaned and polished the cottage like you asked, Euan,' said Pearl. 'There's fresh linen in the hall cupboard.'

Euan noted this and thanked Pearl. He hired her as his housekeeper for his farmhouse. Pearl worked as a housekeeper for several clients in the area.

Gordon bought the strawberry jam he'd come in for, and Pearl remained to talk to Minnie while Euan picked up the necessary groceries and then left the ladies to chat.

Striding back across his field carrying the shopping, Euan breathed in the sea breeze as it blew over the landscape. He sensed a tinge of hope in the air, or perhaps his mind was still reeling from the sound of Poppy's lovely voice, and the interest she seemed to show that he was single and apparently handsome. Unlucky in love, he definitely was. But maybe his luck was about to change for the better?

CHAPTER TWO

The first glimpse of the sea shimmering in the distance bolstered Poppy's confidence that she'd done the right thing. Taking a chance on leaving her shared flat in the city behind and driving to a new and hopefully better life in the cottage filled her with a mix of excitement and expectation.

Euan's advertisement had included a link to photographs of the cottage and it looked so quaint and cosy. If it was even half as comfortable as it looked, she'd made the right decision to embark on a fresh start here.

Recently, she'd been trying to force herself out of the rut she was in, and was determined to take a chance on things — lots of things, like taking on the lease of the cottage, giving up her secure but boring job that held no proper prospects. She'd made a huge mistake dating the boss of the management company. No more mistakes like that whopper she told herself. Romance wasn't on her agenda. Getting her embroidery business up and running was her main priority.

For the past year she'd built up quite a lucrative little sideline selling her embroidery patterns, some made into kits. It had reached a level where her 'real job' as her ex called it was an interruption to her embroidery business. Many a morning she'd wanted to set up her sewing instead of trudging into the office for another day of meetings and endless emails. She always looked forward to going home and stitching in the evenings. These were her fun times. Busy, but fun, and seeing the orders racking up in her online shop filled her with energy rather than tired her out. She'd sew until the early hours, unaware of the time as she enjoyed her embroidery designing and stitching more than anything.

In the distance she saw the fields along the coastline. Trees arched over the road as she wound her way down towards the sea. A smattering of leaves were starting to turn to bronze and autumn tones as the summer faded to make way for the new season. She'd always loved the colours of the autumn and many of her recent embroidery patterns were designed to be stitched with shades of copper, gold and rich chestnut threads.

9

Sunlight flickered through the branches of the trees, and she breathed in the fresh sea air wafting in the car window as she navigated her way down the narrow road, following the route Euan had emailed.

'You can do this,' she assured herself as the butterflies in her stomach threatened to disturb her calm. 'And you have the quilting bee to join,' she added as a bonus.

The full view of the coastline made her blink and slow down to admire it. There was the tiny harbour, just as she'd imagined, with a row of little shops, some converted cottages, all painted in pastel shades of pink, lemon and eau–de–nil that looked like her recent embroidery cottage designs. A handful of boats were anchored in the harbour, adding to the feeling that this was the perfect location to live and work. A patchwork of fields rose up from the coast towards the trees, including Euan's flower fields.

It was time to be more adventurous she told herself as she saw her first glimpse of the cottage. Set in part of one of the fields, it looked so pretty with its pale pink window frames and door. The whitewashed walls had an array of wisteria and other flowers climbing up the exterior. From the photographs, she recognised the pink flowering tree beside the cottage, and the pink clematis covered arch that led through to the back garden. Bees buzzed around the lilac and lavender while butterflies fluttered through the pansies and cornflowers.

She drove up to the entrance of the field, a pathway that barely allowed her car through. Flowers and greenery brushed against the car as she headed for the cottage, and the floral scent mingled with the sea air.

She parked her car in the garden and stepped out, easing the tension from her shoulders after the long drive. She'd meant to stop a couple of times for a tea break, but instead she'd kept on driving, her eagerness to reach the cottage far outweighing the need for a cuppa. Her silky chestnut hair shone in the late afternoon sunlight and she breathed deeply while taking in how perfect the cottage looked.

No one was around and she walked across the lawn that was edged with flower beds to peer in one of the windows. The sunlight reflected on the glass and she cupper her hands to shade her pale grey eyes from the glare. She could see that the living room had a traditional chintz sofa and chairs, and it appeared to have a real log fire. She could barely contain her excitement. The rent of the cottage was affordable and she had savings to pay for the two months advance rent, and aimed to work hard to make a profit from her embroidery work.

She was so deep in thought, planning how she'd make this whole adventure work, that she didn't notice the tall, handsome man approach her.

'You must be Poppy,' he announced trying and failing not to startle her.

She spun around and looked up into his smiling face. A handsome face indeed with gorgeous hazel eyes. Minnie's description of him was entirely accurate. Her heart quickened and she reacted to his sheer masculinity. His clothes were classy. He blended into the scenery and yet...a man like him definitely stood out from the crowd.

He was looking at her...

She blinked, realising she'd been too steeped in thought and hadn't replied. A blush rose across her cheeks as she tried to sound calm and assured. 'Yes, you must be Euan.' She extended her hand and he accepted it, enveloping hers with his strong grasp.

'I was hoping you'd arrive before it got dark,' he explained.

She watched his smile fade and his firm lips show a hint of concern.

'The road is a bit tricky to find in the evenings if you've never been here,' he continued. 'But once you get used to the lay of the land, it's easy to navigate.' He glanced up towards the trees. 'The forest deepens further up on the hill and I hoped you wouldn't take a wrong turn and end up driving round in circles through the trees.'

They both paused for a second, looking at each other, and she assessed he approved of her. She'd worn a pair of black trousers that she often wore to the office, and teamed them with a light pink blouse. Her outfit suited her slender but shapely figure. Her makeup was minimal and emphasised her grey eyes and attractive pale features. She'd never had a tendency to blush, but for some reason she felt her cheeks flush when she looked at Euan. Maybe she was in need of a cup of tea after all.

Euan dangled a set of keys and stepped up to the cottage. 'People round here rarely lock their doors, but I thought I'd secure the cottage for your arrival.'

He turned the key and pushed open the front door, standing aside and gesturing to her. 'After you.'

Poppy nodded up at him, dipped below his arm as he held the door open, and estimated that he must be over six feet tall. She was wearing pumps and he towered over her.

'I've stocked the fridge with fresh milk and a few bits and pieces to tide you over until you can sort out your shopping,' he said, leading the way through to the kitchen at the back of the cottage. The kitchen decor was white and blue, a theme matching the ceramic teapots and dishes on display on the old fashioned wooden dresser that someone had painted eggshell blue. Even the white lace curtains were tied with blue ribbons.

'This is pretty. It's vintage and yet...modern too.'

'The farmer and his wife, the previous owners, kept the original furnishings when they let the cottage to holidaymakers, but they added all the modern necessities.' He looked around him. 'It really is very nice.'

'Have you owned it long?'

'No, I purchased the field recently and the cottage was part of the deal. I never intended being a landlord, but I thought that renting it out, at least until I decide what I'll eventually do with it, was a sensible idea.'

Euan looked like the sensible sort, she thought to herself. And so handsome. She cut herself short from further admiration of Euan. Romance wasn't on her agenda. And besides, everything was sort of temporary at the moment.

He put the keys down on the kitchen table, and checked that everything was in order for her. He looked almost too big for the little kitchen.

'I need your details so I can send you the rent for the first two months in advance,' she said.

This was the first time that Euan looked uncomfortable. 'One month would be fine, and you don't have to pay until you're ready.' He'd no idea if she needed time to settle her finances, and money wasn't an issue with him. Quite the opposite. Having her looking after the cottage was a weight off his shoulders. He didn't want it to sit empty, or have the obligation of checking it every other day, so she was doing him a favour until he decided if he'd sell the cottage or continue to rent it out.

'One month in advance? I thought it was two,' she clarified.

'One.' He smiled tightly. He was tempted not to take any of this young woman's hard earned money, but felt this would look awkward for someone leasing out a property. 'I'll email my details later.'

Having settled the financial hurdle, he gave her a quick tour of the cottage.

'This is the bedroom.' He stepped inside. 'A nice big double bed—' He suddenly realised this sounded all wrong. 'What I mean is...it's not a single bed.' It was Euan's turn to look flustered.

'It's fine,' she assured him. 'I know what you mean.'

'Great,' he said and strode out into the hall. 'The linen cupboard has plenty of fresh sheets and towels. And there's a smaller room at the back that used to be a single bedroom, but I had it cleared. It has a chest of drawers and a wardrobe. Maybe it would be useful for storing your work or stock or whatever you need.'

'Yes, it would be handy for stashing my fabric and other items for packing my embroidery kits off to customers. It would keep the living room tidy.'

'I'll give you one of the large tables from my farmhouse for your packing.'

'Thank you, I'd appreciate that.'

He led her through to the living room that ran the length of the cottage from the front to the back garden. A glass door opened out on to a small patio, and the large back garden was bordered by a floral hedgerow.

'The garden is so pretty,' she remarked. 'I love roses, and wisteria is one of my favourite flowers — and the climbing clematis on the garden arch is perfect.'

'You certainly know your flowers,' he said.

'I'm no expert like you, but I've had to learn about flowers as they're a large part of my embroidery designs. I never had a garden or even a window box at my flat. Everything is gleaned from books or online.'

'Well, now you can study them for real,' he announced. 'And you're welcome to pick any flowers you need from my fields.' He pointed to the adjoining field where his large farmhouse was situated, tucked into the far side of the field. 'That's one of my main fields, and you can pick what you need from there too. I have three fields and now this one makes a fourth.'

'I wouldn't want to waste your flowers,' she told him.

'There are hundreds of blooms. A few picked by you won't spoil the crops.'

'That's very kind of you, and it would be handy because I'm designing a new range of floral patterns for thread painting.'

'Thread painting?' he said.

'It's an embroidery technique using long and short stitches to create quite a realistic effect.'

'It sounds interesting.'

She reeled off the various flowers she planned to design. 'Everything from bluebells to zinnia. I've finished the bluebells, cornflowers and forget–me–nots. Blue flowers are great for my embroidery patterns.'

'You must show me when you're not too busy,' he said, and then started to head out, aware that he was lingering and becoming more interested in Poppy and her work than he'd anticipated.

'I will,' she confirmed, walking with him.

His tall stature seemed to fill the cottage hallway. She noticed his broad shoulders tapered down to a toned torso and long legs. Not that she was admiring him. Not at all she lied to herself.

'I'll help carry your bags inside,' he said, striding over to her car.

'Thanks.'

He grabbed a load of her belongings and lifted them with ease into the cottage while she lugged one of her large suitcases.

He was already heading back out to pick up more when he saw her hoisting the suitcase up the path.

He lifted it for her, and smiled. 'What have you got in this — bars of gold?'

She laughed. 'I wish. It's my cutting equipment and artwork items.'

'Artwork? You're an artist?' he asked while continuing to carry the case into the hallway.

'I draw all my own embroidery designs — flowers, bees, butterflies, birds, various creatures, and cottages. I sketch my designs and then ink them into finished artwork for the embroidery patterns. It's part of the design process. A large part of my work.'

He nodded, realising that of course she'd need the artwork for the patterns. Somehow he'd pictured her embroidery work would comprise only of sewing.

'There's an antique writing desk in my farmhouse that I never use. You're welcome to have it if it's of any use to you.'

'A writing desk?' The spark of interest in her tone was clear.

'Yes, it's one of those vintage pieces with a roll down front, a desk area for writing and drawing and dookits for pens, paper—'

'I'll take it. If you don't use it.'

'I'm not the artistic type. And I have a desk in my study.'

She smiled at him, and his heart squeezed just looking at her.

'I'll have the desk and table delivered to the cottage tomorrow, or later this evening if you prefer.'

'Tomorrow would be fine.'

He smiled and nodded. 'Well, I'll leave you to settle in.' He headed outside.

She walked with him to the front door.

He started to walk away and then paused. 'Minnie told me to remind you that the quilting bee is on this evening, so if you're not too tired or busy settling in, you're welcome to join them.'

'I'd love to.' The enthusiasm in her voice was obvious.

'They meet at seven in Gordon's tea shop.' He indicated towards the shops along at the harbour nearby. 'Tea, cake and lashings of gossip are included.' He smiled at her. A warm, sexy smile.

She smiled back at him. 'Thank you, Euan. I appreciate the kind welcome.'

With a casual wave he walked away.

She stood in the cottage doorway watching him cut across her garden and head towards his farmhouse. Whatever she'd imagined Euan would be, he'd exceeded her expectations. But then she remembered...a stab of reality bringing her to her senses. This was how her relationships in the past always started. When it came to picking nice, kind, reliable and good looking men, her senses were wired all wrong. She wasn't here to make another huge mistake. Oh no, she scolded herself. Romance was on the back burner for the foreseeable future. Maybe even longer than that.

15

She closed the cottage door and went through to the kitchen to make herself a cup of tea and a sandwich. Euan had left a fresh, crusty loaf of bread in the kitchen, and on checking the fridge, there was red cheddar cheese tempting her to make a doorstep of a sandwich and enjoy this while settling in.

And so that's what she did.

The cottage felt secure and so quiet. She loved the quietude, something the city never provided. The thick stone walls of the sturdily built cottage shielded her from the elements. As she sat on one of the comfy, old fashioned chairs in the living room, gazing out the window at the sea and the fields, she felt she'd done the right thing leaving the past behind.

Finishing her tea and sandwich, she unpacked the heavy case that included all her botanical sketch books and artwork items and stacked them on the bookcase shelves.

Then she sat beside the fireplace, wondering if she'd light the fire in the hearth later that evening. Maybe the evening wouldn't be cold enough to merit lighting it, but she loved the idea of sitting beside a cosy fire, a real log fire, something she'd never had before in any of the flats she'd lived in.

She gazed again out the window and sighed happily. The sun was refusing to fade to evening without putting on a magnificent display of lilac and blue bands of light across the sky. Did that indicate a storm was brewing? She didn't know.

That sexy voice, the warm smile and lovely hazel eyes of Euan's kept flickering through her mind, despite her efforts not to think about him. Why was an eligible man like him not settled, unmarried? Minnie said he was unlucky in love. Maybe later at the quilting bee she'd find out more about Euan.

A knock on the front door startled her. She peered out the window and saw Euan standing outside. He appeared to be carrying more groceries.

She opened the door to him.

'I realised I hadn't left you enough fresh groceries,' he said, handing her two bags of shopping. 'Minnie selected most of these, and I've added some fruit and cereal.' He indicated that he'd included a box of porridge oats. 'I don't know what you enjoy for breakfast, but personally I love my oats first thing every morning.'

His words hung in the air for a moment and he wished he could unwind what he'd said.

Poppy tried to suppress a smile, and failed.

'What I mean is...I like a bowl of porridge for breakfast,' he clarified awkwardly.

Poppy accepted the groceries and made no comment on his faux pas. 'Thank you for the extra groceries, Euan.' She peered into one of the bags and saw it contained a bag of flour, eggs, baking powder, a jar of strawberry jam, sugar and a tub of glacé cherries. 'All the ingredients to bake a cake.'

'Eh, yes,' he muttered, thinking Minnie must've added those.

'I assume you can cook, a man living on his own.'

'I can. My hearty stews are a mainstay.' This was true. Any recipe where he could throw everything into the one pot or casserole dish and let it cook itself.

Before he could tell her that cooking wasn't really something he was adept at, she was complimenting him.

'Cooking is a life skill that men like yourself should have. I've often thought that a man with cooking skills is very impressive. Particularly if they can bake.'

Euan smiled tightly. 'Definitely.'

'So you can bake cakes?' she said hopefully. 'Victoria sponge is my favourite. There's nothing quite like home baking.'

'Indeed. I'll eh...rustle one up for you if you'd like,' he offered stupidly. Just being near her sent his senses haywire. She'd tied her silky, shoulder–length hair into a ponytail and it emphasised her beautiful face, soft lips and those pale grey eyes...

'That would be great. With strawberry or raspberry jam. I love both.'

'Duly noted,' he muttered, and then hurried away, mentally kicking himself for letting her think he could bake. He'd never baked anything successfully. Cooking casseroles, stews and scrambled eggs were his culinary limits.

CHAPTER THREE

Euan headed home to his farmhouse with a heart heavy with guilt. What a stupid thing to have promised her. Bake a Victoria sponge cake? He needed a plan to wangle out of it or...he could genuinely give it a go. He was sure there were recipe books somewhere in one of the kitchen cupboards.

The beautiful, two–storey farmhouse was steeped in greenery, with climbing roses and other flowers clambering up the walls and arching over the windows. It faced the sea, and one of Euan's favourite times of the day was the early evening when the view of the seascape looked like a painting. The view changed with the seasons, and even on winter nights in the twilight's glow, the sense of calm eased away any stress of a hard working day. Not that Euan shirked hard work. Not at all. Brought up to be awake at dawn when the dew still sparkled on the flowers, he enjoyed working outside in his fields. He travelled to give talks on his flowers, but was always glad when it was time to come home. He'd never been a wanderer. Definitely a homebody. The flower farming life suited him perfectly. If anything was missing, it was a special woman to share it with.

Inside the farmhouse the decor was bright and airy, though very traditional. The large windows let in plenty of light, and the polished wooden floors were scattered with light, neutral coloured rugs — pale grey, beige and soft gold. His love of autumnal tones was reflected in his study where a solid oak desk that was older than the farmhouse itself stood in the centre of the room. His computer was a necessity he endured. All his business files and documents were stored in antique cabinets whose veneers were so shiny they looked like glass.

The dining room was light and airy and extended through to the kitchen. A sturdy wooden table was his second desk where he'd attend to correspondence and consider cultivating new plants each season while eating his meals alone. But he wasn't lonely. Not in a community like this.

He started to open the kitchen cupboards where he thought the recipe books were stashed. Yes, there they were, lined up on one of the shelves. He pulled out the book he recognised, one he'd used when attempting to make eggnog for Christmas. It was a total disaster that he'd poured down the sink and opted for a shot of whisky with his Christmas pudding. But he wasn't much of a drinker, preferring a cup of tea.

He sat down at the table and flicked through the book.

A note he'd written to himself a while ago tumbled out from the pages. *Don't bake anything*, the note warned him. He sighed wearily, remembering the chocolate cake fiasco. Something best forgotten along with the eggnog. Hardly the enticement he needed to bolster his confidence that he really could bake a cake.

A glance at the book's index showed there was a recipe for a traditional Victoria sponge cake. He flicked to the page and skim read the instructions. It didn't seem too difficult, and if he hurried up he'd be able to buy the necessary ingredients from Minnie's shop before she closed for the evening.

'Baking a cake are you?' Minnie asked, sounding surprised as he placed the items on the counter. Self–raising flour, baking powder, caster and icing sugar, eggs, butter, strawberry and raspberry jam. She was used to Euan's usual shopping list. Yes, he was up to something. The guilt showed on his face.

'Just picking up a few extras this evening, Minnie.' He tried to sound chirpy, but she knew he was up to no good. She knew.

He paid for the items.

She handed them over in a bag, quickly adding a roll of greaseproof paper.

He took the bag without comment and started to head out.

'Whatever you're up to, Euan,' she warned him, 'don't be causing any trouble for Poppy.'

Pretending not to hear her, he waved cheerily without glancing back. 'Enjoy your quilting bee tonight, Minnie.'

He scuttled out the door like a shot before she could saying anything else, trailing the weight of the guilt behind him.

Minnie locked the shop door and turned the notice to *closed*.

'Euan's definitely up to something,' she said to Bracken, and then started to get her things ready for the quilting bee.

As cooking disasters go, Euan scored a ten on the total failure scale. Not only was his Victoria sponge burned around one edge, he'd managed to bake a cake that was flat and wonky. In some alternate universe this might merit a gold star for achieving the impossible. Thankfully, he'd used the greaseproof paper Minnie had given him to line the baking tin, so he was able to tip the culinary catastrophe into the bin without having to scrape it out with a spatula. It landed with a dull thud.

He closed the recipe book, slipped his warning note into the pages where he hoped he'd never venture again, tucked the book back on the shelf and shut the cupboard door.

While the kettle boiled for tea, he poured himself a dram of whisky. Sometimes life merited it. Tonight was one of those nights.

And that's when he had an idea.

In the tea shop kitchen trouble was brewing along with the tea.

Gordon frowned when he saw Euan scuttle in.

'I've got myself into a pickle,' Euan confessed while Gordon prepared two large pots of tea for the quilting bee ladies.

'What have you done?' Gordon asked casually, assuming it was something trivial.

'I've sort of told Poppy that I can bake.'

Gordon laughed.

'What will I do?'

'Tell her the truth.'

'I can't. She'll think I'm an idiot.'

Gordon smiled at him.

'Okay, so it was an idiotic thing to say, but she got the wrong impression when I gave her groceries that included flour and baking stuff.'

Gordon paused and looked at Euan. 'What's happened to you? You're always so in control. You're gibbering like a love struck eejit.'

'It's Poppy. I didn't expect her to be so...attractive. I can't stop thinking about her. I feel discombobulated.'

Gordon tried not to laugh.

'It's not funny.'

'It is.'

'I came to you for baking advice. Can you give my any tips on baking a Victoria sponge cake?'

'Do you know how to sift flour into a bowl?'

'No, of course not.'

'Cream butter and sugar lightly?'

A clueless look from Euan.

Gordon reached for one of his recipe books and flicked through it. 'Read this. Could you do this? It's a traditional Victoria sponge cake.'

Euan skim read the recipe and confessed to his recent disaster.

'It's not a difficult cake to bake. What did your cake look like?' Gordon tried to establish where Euan had gone wrong.

Euan considered for a moment and then described it. 'The last time I saw anything like it, I was watching a film about aliens.'

Gordon grabbed the book off him and tucked it back on the shelf. 'You're clueless, aren't you?'

'Well, yes, when it comes to baking cakes.'

Taking charge of the situation, Gordon pointed to the cupboard. 'Grab an apron, wash your hands and let's get you trained up.'

'Tonight?' Euan checked the time in a mild panic. 'The quilting bee ladies will be arriving any minute.'

'They will, but tonight, you're going to be my little helper. I could do with a pair of extra hands this evening. It's been one of those busy days and I haven't even got the tea brewed yet.'

'But the ladies will see me,' Euan protested.

'Not if you're hidden in the kitchen. They don't come through here. They'll be busy sewing in the function room. They'll never know you're here.'

'Are you sure? Poppy's going to be at the bee.'

Gordon studied Euan. 'You've got it bad, buddy.'

'What?'

'You know what. Poppy's got you all in a tizzy. I understand. I've been there myself. I remember how I was affected when Abby arrived here. I really liked Abby.'

'So did I. We all liked Abby.'

'Yes, but you didn't feel inclined to become a baker to impress her, or act like an eejit.'

'No, I left those merits to you.'

'If you're going to be cheeky, you can teach yourself to bake,' Gordon told him.

'No, no, sorry. I'm just—'

'A wee bit smitten with the new girl.'

Euan sighed heavily. 'There's something about her...the moment I met her I felt...well, I've never felt like this before. And I barely know her.'

'Time has nothing to do with it. The first time I met Eila I couldn't think straight afterwards. I took her a cake as a welcoming present. She'd opened her dress shop. I was just being friendly. I didn't expect her to look so beautiful.'

'But it worked out for you, didn't it? You and Eila are together now. You're going to marry her, aren't you?'

'That's my plan.'

The sound of the ladies arriving, chattering and giggling, resonated through to the kitchen.

'Hurry up, Euan. Apron on, hands scrubbed and let's get you baking.'

Euan unhooked a clean white apron and put it on. 'How many straps do you need?' he complained, trying to tie the numerous long strands around his waist.

Gordon put his tea preparation aside and tied them for him. 'Grab a hat and put it on too, just in case any of the ladies wander through.'

Euan's eyes widened. 'You said they never came through here.'

'They don't, but you're jinxing things, so stick it on and tuck that telltale mop of hair in.'

Euan shoved the chef's white hat on and tucked his burnished gold hair inside it. A few unruly strands stuck out, but his disguise would work he told himself. It would. Definitely. Maybe.

'Hurry up and wash your hands,' Gordon insisted.

Euan washed his hands, muttering as he did so.

'Attitude, Euan, it's all about attitude too, so buck up and start breaking the eggs into a bowl.'

Poppy walked along the narrow path that led down to the harbour and esplanade. She'd packed embroidery items in her sewing bag. These included copies of her bumblebee pattern that she intended giving to the quilting bee members. Pretty cottage patterns with floral garden settings were a recent addition to her design portfolio. Most of her embroideries fitted into six or seven inch hoops, and she'd popped some of them into the bag, along with the patterns and a box of thread. Two cottage embroideries were almost finished, and the third only had the roof stitched with crewel wool to create a textured effect. One hoop had a bee that she'd started and she thought it would be ideal for embroidering during the evening.

She wore a sky blue blouse with her black trousers and a white cardigan rather than a jacket as it was a mild night. She'd brushed her hair smooth and wore in down around her shoulders.

The early evening sunlight shone across the calm sea making it look like the water had been chromed with a layer of bronze. Far in the distance she saw the soft focus outline of the islands. A few lights twinkled on the horizon and further along the coastline where other little communities were situated. She breathed it all in, so fresh, exciting and new. Moments like this were made for perfect memories. She would remember her first night here, heading to the tea shop, armed with her sewing bag that she'd sewn herself and embroidered with flowers and butterflies.

She felt tempted to go for a walk along the shore but she didn't want to be late for the quilting bee or trail sand into the tea shop from her pumps. Another time, she promised herself and continued along the esplanade to the tea shop.

The windows of the vintage style tea shop were aglow with lights and she could see ladies going in, carrying bags and chattering excitedly.

She hurried to join them, eager to meet Minnie and the other ladies.

Drawn in by the welcoming atmosphere and delicious aroma of baking, she saw that there were customers seated at small tables at the front of the tea shop. The glass counter and display cabinets were filled with cakes, scones, savoury onion flans and cheese pastries. One cabinet had a tempting range of Gordon's chocolates, truffles, butterscotch, Scottish tablet and fudge. A supper menu offered Scotch broth and lentil soup with crusty bread. The function room at the back was busy with ladies setting up their sewing. The chatter was combined with laughter.

'Poppy!' a woman called through to her. Minnie had seen her standing there holding an embroidered sewing bag, and rightly assumed that Poppy had arrived. 'We're through here.' Minnie waved her to come in.

Smiling, and feeling slightly nervous to meet the other ladies, Poppy walked through the tea shop to the function room. Glass doors opened out into the tea shop's back garden, and one of the doors was jammed open to let fresh air in. The atmosphere was cosy, friendly and alive with activity.

'I'm Minnie,' the familiar voice said, standing up to welcome her. 'I'm glad you could make it this evening. We've lots of gossip and sewing planned.'

'Thanks for inviting me,' said Poppy, unfamiliar with the fuss the ladies were making of her, the smiling faces, clearly happy to welcome a newcomer to their already busy bee.

Poppy was seated between Minnie and Pearl right in the hub of the bee. Sewing machines set up on tables at the edges of the function room whirred with the sounds of quilts being made. A couple of ladies were working on their knitting and crochet.

'Gordon should be bringing the tea through soon so you'll get a cuppa and cake,' Minnie told her, before making the round of introductions to the other members.

Poppy smiled and acknowledged everyone.

'I see you've got an embroidered sewing bag,' Pearl remarked. 'Did you make it yourself?'

'I did. I love sewing, and if something can be embroidered, I'll embroider it.'

'You're like me,' commented Judy, a woman of similar age to Minnie and Pearl, with light blonde hair and a confident manner. 'I love embroidering motifs on to my clothes.'

'Judy and her husband Jock own the bar restaurant next door to the tea shop,' said Minnie. 'Judy's an expert dressmaker.'

'I worked as a dressmaker before I married Jock,' Judy explained. 'If you ever need a dress, my wardrobes are full of them. I buy too many bargains and make them as a hobby, a sideline. Jock's given up curtailing me. He bought me another wardrobe for my birthday.'

The ladies giggled, and Poppy made a mental note that if she needed a dress she knew where to go.

'I'm not into dressmaking,' said Poppy. 'Maybe one day, but there aren't enough hours in the day to do all the embroidery I want.'

'I know how you feel,' Minnie sympathised. 'I love my grocery shop, but sometimes I'd happily do my quilting all day.'

Several heads nodded in agreement.

'Do quite a few of you run your craft businesses from your cottages and houses around here?' Poppy asked them as the sewing continued around her.

'Most of us do,' Pearl told her. 'I'm a local housekeeper for quite a few folk, including Euan. He hired me to give your cottage an extra clean and tidy. But I sell my quilts and make a nice wee profit from it.'

'The quilting bee has a website,' said Minnie. 'We recently set it up so members could sell their quilts and other craft items.'

'We've a quilting bee kitty that funds the upkeep of the website,' explained Judy. 'I update it. I run the bar restaurant's website, so it's easy for me to do.'

'The quilting kitty, the small fund we have for our bee membership, has been making a tidy profit and we all benefit from being able to advertise our items on the website,' said Pearl.

'I'd love to join,' Poppy told them. The membership was minimal and it was agreed that Poppy was welcome.

'It's parting with the quilts and other things I make that's the problem,' Minnie confessed. 'The hours, weeks or months of work that goes into making a full–size quilt...well, you become attached to it. Then when you've got a buyer, it's hard to let it go. I've got a stash of quilts that I just can't part with.' Minnie indicated that the pile was high.

'Get yourself another wardrobe,' Judy said jokingly. 'That's what I do.'

The light–hearted chatter circled around Poppy and she felt part of the bee rather than the new member.

'Tell us about your embroidery work,' Minnie encouraged Poppy.

'I've been embroidering since I was a wee girl,' Poppy began. 'A couple of years ago I set up my own website to sell my patterns online. I kept my job at the management company in Glasgow and stitched in the evenings and at weekends. Eventually, the demand for my patterns was hard to keep up with, and I decided to take a chance and make it into a business.'

The ladies bombarded Poppy with questions, interested in what she created.

'I design all my own patterns from my original artwork,' Poppy explained. 'Mainly flowers, bees, butterflies, birds, dragonflies.

Lately, I've been designing cottages.' She showed them her embroideries.

'These are beautiful,' Minnie remarked, passing them around to let the other ladies see Poppy's work.

'What type of thread do you use?' one of the ladies asked.

'Stranded cotton, and some patterns include crewel wool. The cottage designs have their roofs stitched with crewel wool.'

'I'd like a go at crewel embroidery,' Pearl remarked. 'I'll need to try one of your cottage patterns.'

'I brought some patterns with me.' Poppy brought them out of her bag. She handed a cottage pattern to Pearl.

'Thank you,' said Pearl. 'I'll buy this one.'

'No, I didn't want to turn up empty handed tonight,' Poppy told them. 'And this is one of my bee embroidery patterns. I thought it would be appropriate for the bee night.' She handed several copies of the pattern to Minnie.

'That's very generous of you, Poppy,' said Minnie.

'Maybe you can share them around the members,' Poppy told Minnie.

There was a flurry of interest in the patterns.

'Is the bee satin stitched?' Judy asked.

'It's thread painted, using single strands of cotton thread and long and short stitches.' Poppy explained.

'Thread painting,' said Judy. 'I'd like to try that.'

Quite a few of the members were interested in the thread painted bee pattern, and Poppy was bombarded with questions.

'There are instructional videos on my website that show the process,' Poppy told them. 'Long and short stitch is so handy for embroidering the bee. It's really just lots and lots of straight stitches used to shade the bee. Some of you will have heard it called needle painting or silk shading.'

Several members were nodding and started to look up Poppy's website for details.

'What size of hoop do I need?' asked Judy.

'A six or seven inch is ideal,' said Poppy. 'I used cotton fabric and traced the bee pattern on with a pencil. Then I added a piece of cotton backing fabric to give it more substance before I put it in the hoop for sewing.'

'Could I use linen?' one of the ladies asked.

'Yes, linen or cotton linen mixes are fabrics that I use as well,' Poppy told her. 'The pattern includes suggestions for fabric, hoops and needle sizes as well as the colours of threads I used to make the finished bee.'

'I'm definitely going to give this a go,' said Judy, putting the pattern in her bag. She stood up. 'I'm just popping through to buy a bag of Gordon's new white chocolate truffles. I promised Jock I'd bring him back a treat.' And off she went, hurrying through to the front of the tea shop.

'Chocolate truffles?' said Poppy. 'They sound delicious.'

'Too delicious,' said Pearl. 'Gordon's cakes and confectionery are so tasty. He's always creating new flavours, and of course, we enjoy tasting them all, don't we, girls?'

There were nods and smiles all round.

'You'll meet Gordon when he brings the tea through,' Minnie told Poppy. 'He's very nice.' Minnie thought that Gordon was a bit later than usual bringing through the tea, but assumed he was icing Poppy's name on a cake.

Poppy admired the tea shop's decor. 'I love the vintage look of the tea shop. The pink and amber glass shades on those lamps are gorgeous.'

'The lamps are genuine vintage,' said Minnie. 'Gordon made an effort to blend as many authentic pieces with new items to give the tea shop a wonderful atmosphere.'

'Has he owned it long?' asked Poppy.

'No, not too long. He's another newcomer, like yourself, but settled now and dating a nice young woman who also moved here recently.'

'Gordon swims every morning in the sea,' Pearl told Poppy. 'Keeps himself very fit.'

'I was tempted to go for a walk along the shore on the way here tonight,' Poppy confessed.

'Are you a swimmer?' Pearl asked her. 'Judy used to be a champion swimmer and she still goes for a dip when the weather's fair.'

'I haven't been swimming in the sea for years.' Poppy sighed, feeling she'd missed out on this. 'Living in the city...' she shrugged. 'But I intend to make up for it. Though I suppose the water is freezing.'

'No, it's okay at this time of year,' said Pearl. 'It's fresh, but wouldn't bite the bahookie off you.'

Poppy laughed, and they continued to chat about embroidery, sewing, quilting, and knitting while waiting for their tea and cake.

'No, Euan, don't over beat your mixture,' Gordon scolded him. 'Leave some air in it so that your cake will rise nice and light.'

Euan adjusted his hat and tried not to feel flustered. 'I'll get the hang of it. I will.'

'Yes, it just takes practice,' said Gordon. 'You're nearly ready to pour your cake mix into the baking tins.'

Euan felt a surge of enthusiasm. 'Okay, I can do this. It's not that difficult when you know how.'

'Exactly. Now don't over do it until I get back. I have to serve up the tea. The ladies will be wondering what's wrong. I'm running late.'

Euan glanced at the cake sitting waiting on a serving trolley. 'I see you've iced Poppy's name on it. Very nice.'

'Do you think I should add a candle?'

'Yes, why not. Let Poppy have a wish.'

Gordon nodded and stuck a pretty pink candle into the cake. 'There, that should do it.'

Neither of them noticed Judy standing at the kitchen door. 'Gordon,' she called to him. 'I've taken the last bag of your white truffles. I'll settle up with you later.' She held the bag up.

'That's fine,' Gordon said, smiling tightly, hoping she hadn't noticed Euan.

Euan kept his back to her and feigned being extra busy with his cake mixing.

'I'm running a wee bit late this evening,' Gordon said, sounding guilty. 'It's been one of those busy days. But I've got an extra helper this evening, so I'll be through with the tea and cakes in a minute.' Usually, he wouldn't be training someone to bake and would be tending to the front tea shop counter while zipping back and forth serving the quilting bee ladies.

Judy smiled and nodded. 'Thanks, Gordon. I'll tell the ladies.' She hurried away.

Euan's broad shoulders slumped. 'Do you think Judy recognised me?'

'No, no,' Gordon lied.

CHAPTER FOUR

'I've been caught, haven't I?' Euan said, sounding downhearted.

'Try to look confident, as if you know what you're doing,' Gordon advised.

Euan straightened his shoulders. 'If this cake bakes up well, I won't feel guilty about lying to Poppy, because I will be capable of baking a cake.'

Gordon nodded. 'And I won't be your accomplice.'

They gave each other a high five and then Gordon wheeled the tea trolley through to the function room to face the ladies.

'Wish me luck,' Gordon said as he headed out of the kitchen.

Judy rushed over to the ladies, smiling with mischievous glee. 'You'll never guess who is helping Gordon in the kitchen tonight.'

'I thought he was working on his own,' said Minnie.

'No, someone is busy baking in the kitchen.' Judy's lips curved into a grin.

'I've no idea,' said Minnie.

None of the ladies knew.

'Euan,' Judy announced.

There were astonished looks all round.

'Euan? Are you sure?' said Pearl. 'He can't bake for toffee.'

Judy shrugged and smiled. 'Well he's kitted out in his whites and seems to be helping bake cakes.'

Minnie bit her lip. 'He bought flour, baking powder and other stuff for making a cake from my shop just before closing.'

Pearl blinked. 'Really? I'm surprised he even knew to buy baking powder. He's handless in his own kitchen.'

Judy sighed. 'I wish I'd known he could bake. There's many a busy night at the bar restaurant when we've been short staffed. I'd have asked him to help us out instead of sitting in his farmhouse plaiting his bulbs. Now that I know he's handy with a spatula, I wonder if he'd help Jock and me out this weekend. The big party night to celebrate the start of autumn is on and I could do with someone to muck in.'

'I'll help you,' Minnie offered, as did a few of the other ladies.

'No, I want us all to dress up and enjoy the party. Euan's never been a party animal, and you've seen what he's like at the ceilidh dancing. All kilt and no clue.'

'I suppose you could ask him,' said Minnie.

'Ask who what?' Gordon quipped, arriving with their tea and cake.

'Euan,' said Judy. 'To help with the catering at our party night this weekend.'

Gordon almost choked.

'Are you okay?' Minnie asked him.

'Yes, just needing a sip of water to wet my whistle,' said Gordon, hiding his reaction.

'Ask him if he'd be interested,' Judy told Gordon. 'Unless he's too busy helping you.'

'I'll ask him,' Gordon managed to mutter while stifling his laughter. 'But I think he's planning on going to the party night and eh...asking Poppy to go with him.' He wondered why he'd uttered this, but it was out before he could rethink it.

Poppy blushed. 'Euan's going to invite me to the party?'

'Yes,' Gordon lied.

'Oh, we've got another wee romance brewing,' Minnie said, delighted.

The other ladies joined in the warmth of the moment.

'Euan can bake,' said Poppy. 'He promised to bake me a Victoria sponge.'

'It just shows you that you can know someone for years, and not know all their quirks and abilities,' said Pearl, prepared to accept that Euan could bake and she just didn't know about it.

Gordon served up the tea and cake, and then presented the special chocolate cake to Poppy.

'Welcome to our quilting bee, Poppy,' Minnie announced. The ladies clapped and smiled.

Poppy was taken aback that her name was iced on the cake. 'I didn't expect a cake'.

Gordon sparked a match and lit the candle. 'Make a wish.'

Poppy took a deep breath, closed her eyes and wished with all her heart that she would be happy here and find friendship. She blew out the candle, and everyone cheered.

31

Gordon cut a slice of the cake and put it on a plate for Poppy. 'I hope your wish comes true.'

Minnie winked at the ladies. 'I wonder what she wished for?'

Poppy giggled. 'I can't tell you or it won't come true.'

The playful mood of the evening continued while they enjoyed their tea and cakes.

Gordon went back through to the kitchen to find Euan wondering if he should pour the mixture into one tin or two.

'Two tins. You're going to impress Poppy by giving her a big one.'

Euan smirked.

'A large Victoria sponge cake,' Gordon clarified, and then they both laughed.

'I better warn you,' said Gordon. 'Judy wants to hire your culinary services at the bar restaurant this weekend. They're short staffed for their party night.'

Euan guffawed. 'You're joking.'

'Nope. They all think you're a whiz in the kitchen, including Poppy. She was sticking up for you, telling them you'd promised to bake her a cake.'

Euan shook his head in dismay. 'What did you tell Judy?'

'I said you had other plans.'

Euan sensed that Gordon had said more than that.

Gordon relented and confessed. 'I sort of hinted that you intended asking Poppy to go with you to the party night.'

Euan's eyes widened in panic.

'Sorry, I don't know why I said it. It just sort of blurted out before I could think it through.'

Euan couldn't berate Gordon for this as he knew how easy it was to make stupid promises.

'What was Poppy's reaction?' Euan asked.

'She was blushing but looked flattered. Then I got her to blow out the candle and make a wish.'

'What did she wish for?'

Gordon shrugged. 'I don't know. Wishes are secret, but she was still blushing and the ladies were hinting that a romance was brewing between you and Poppy.'

One part of Euan's brain felt fried from all the guilt and lies, while the other part cheered. 'Maybe I should ask her.'

'You'd better, or we're going to be in a bigger pickle than we are now.'

Euan took a deep breath. 'Okay, I'll ask her.' He straightened his chef's hat and adjusted his apron. 'What else do you serve up to the ladies?'

Gordon handed him a plate of chocolate truffles. 'I usually tempt them with my truffles.'

Euan took charge of them. 'My turn to tempt them tonight.' Steadying himself, he headed through to the function room hoping the chef whites made him look like the adept baker he wished he was.

Minnie nudged Poppy. 'Here comes Euan.'

'Doesn't he look handsome in his hat and apron,' Pearl murmured.

The ladies agreed, and watched as the tall and handsome figure leaned down, offering the plate to Poppy. 'Can I tempt you with a truffle?'

Poppy smiled and picked one up and tasted it. 'This is delicious.'

Euan smiled, not saying he'd made them, but not discarding the credit either.

'If you're not busy this weekend,' he said to Poppy, 'would you like to go with me to the party night at the bar restaurant?'

'I'd love to,' Poppy said, smiling at him.

Euan nodded and smiled at her. She kept blushing, and he hoped it was because she liked him too. No more silly lies from now on, he said to himself. Then he remembered about the cake and the fact that he couldn't really bake or cook very well. But despite the chaos and trouble he'd caused, he'd enjoyed learning to bake a cake. Maybe he'd learn a few more baking skills from Gordon to add to his recipe repertoire.

Euan went back through to the kitchen.

Gordon was making more tea and arranging cupcakes on a cake stand.

'What did Poppy say?' Gordon asked him.

'She said yes.' Euan sounded taken back. 'She's agreed to go with me to the party night.'

'As a date?'

Euan shrugged and adjusted his chef's hat. 'I'm not sure.'

'You'd better clarify the situation.'

'No, I'm quitting while I'm ahead.'

'You do know that there's ceilidh dancing,' Gordon warned him.

Euan's heart sank. 'Oh.'

'Jock will give you some extra lessons.'

'He shouted at me the last time for burling the wrong way.'

'Och, don't fuss, just get a bit of practise in. The chances are that Poppy can't ceilidh dance either.'

'That's true. We could skirl around the dance floor and just have fun.'

'Precisely. It'll be a fun night.'

'Are you going with Eila?'

'She's away on a fashion design course and won't be back for a couple of weeks, but I'll pop in after I've closed the tea shop for the night.'

Euan glanced at the cake tins. 'I suppose I'd better bake my cake.'

'Pour the mixture between the two tins and pop them in the oven,' Gordon instructed him.

Euan did as he was told and closed the glass door of the oven, peering through at his achievement.

'It'll be about twenty minutes before they're ready. Start mixing your buttercream filling, and remember where you went wrong before with your cake fiasco.'

Euan rattled off the list of things he needed to get right. 'Read the recipe properly before doing anything. Make sure I have all the right ingredients including baking powder. Sift the flour to put air in it, don't dump it into the bowl straight from the bag. Don't over mix everything.'

'And...?' Gordon prompted him.

'Preheat the oven.'

'Well done. Now, when the cakes are ready, take them out of the oven and leave them to cool on a rack. Then add the jam and buttercream filling. Finish with a light dusting of icing sugar.'

As the time wore on, Euan helped Gordon in the kitchen, enjoying the atmosphere and the feeling of learning something new.

'I can see why you love your job,' Euan said to Gordon.

'I've always enjoyed baking. And now that you can whip up a sponge mix, there are other things you can do with it.'

Euan's interest perked up. 'Is there?'

Gordon pointed to the cupcakes he was swirling buttercream on. 'These were made with the same recipe.'

'So all I'd have to do is pour them into wee cake tins.'

Gordon nodded. 'And you could sprinkle in a few chocolate chips.'

Euan's eyes lit up. 'That would definitely impress Poppy. And I like the sound of those myself.'

While Gordon taught Euan more baking skills, the ladies continued to enjoy their quilting bee night.

Poppy demonstrated her thread painting technique on her bee embroidery. She handed the hoop to Pearl. 'Now you try it. Long and short stitches. Just go with the flow, following the directions of the pattern lines.'

Others watched as Pearl began adding stitches to the bee, following Poppy's instructions.

'This is a very handy method to fill the bee's body,' said Pearl. 'And quite realistic.'

'It's a lovely type of embroidery,' Minnie agreed.

'It takes time as there are a lot of long and short stitches,' Poppy explained. 'But I find it quite relaxing.'

'It is,' Pearl agreed. 'Yes, I'll certainly practise this.'

Poppy enjoyed seeing the other members working on their crafts including Minnie making hexies for a quilt.

'Can you make hexies?' Minnie asked her.

'I've never tried, but they look like fun.'

'Here, have a go. I thread baste my hexies and then stitch them together by hand with whip stitches. It's a great way to make a quilt. Someone placed an order for one made from ditsy floral designs, and I've usually got plenty of that type of fabric in my stash.'

As the ladies chatted and learned new skills from each other, the night went in quickly. Before Poppy knew it, the evening was almost done. The ladies started to pack their sewing bags and tidy up to get ready to leave.

'Thank you for a great night,' Poppy told them.

'See you again this time next week?' Minnie asked her.

'Definitely,' said Poppy, wishing she didn't have to wait another week before the next bee.

'Thank you for showing me the thread painting,' said Pearl.

Judy nodded. 'I'm going to check out your videos for more details.'

Poppy paused and then said, 'If any of you want to drop by my cottage, feel free to do so.'

'Are you sure?' said Minnie. 'We wouldn't want to spoil you moving in and getting settled.'

'Not at all. I'd be glad of the company. Pop in if you want,' Poppy offered.

'We're all like that,' Minnie told her. 'My grocery shop is the local hub of gossip, and the door to my cottage is always open to the bee members.'

The ladies nodded in agreement.

'Now that you've got a hot date with Euan for the party,' said Judy, 'do you have a dress to wear? Something with a full skirt for the ceilidh dancing?'

Poppy laughed and blushed. 'I wouldn't call it a hot date, or a date at all, it's just a kind invitation from Euan.'

Euan walked into the full force of the comment as he arrived with a bag of milk chocolate truffles for Judy. Gordon had asked him to give the chocolates to Judy for Jock. His heart stung from the realisation that Poppy didn't consider it a date.

The ladies stopped giggling when they saw Euan's smile fade, before he forced a cheery expression. 'Did you all have a nice evening, ladies?'

'We did,' said Minnie.

He flicked a glance at Poppy.

'I hope you didn't take my remark out of context, Euan,' said Poppy.

'Not at all. I didn't think it was a date, hot or otherwise. I just thought you'd like to go to the party night as it's a tradition to welcome in the new season and you'd enjoy meeting some of the other members of the community.'

It was Poppy's turn to feel the sting of disappointment. Though she wondered why. Getting involved with Euan, or anyone romantically, wasn't in her plans. It was kind of Euan to invite her, and sort of a relief that it wasn't a date. And yet...something in her couldn't help but feel a tinge of sadness.

'So we're still on for the party?' Euan wanted to confirm, sensing the awkwardness.

36

'Yes, of course,' Poppy told him chirpily. Then she turned to Judy. 'I'll take you up on the offer of a dress. I used to love ceilidh dancing when I was younger, and went to Highland dance classes, but then I became so busy at work.'

Euan swallowed his anxiousness. 'So you're experienced in ceilidh and Highland dancing?'

Poppy nodded. 'I even considered competing but...' she shrugged.

'Jock will be delighted to welcome someone as skilled as himself,' Judy trilled. 'Come by whenever you want. Tomorrow if you like, and we'll find you a dress from my wardrobes.'

'If you don't come back by the end of the day, we'll send out a search party,' Minnie joked.

Poppy laughed. 'I'll leave a trail of breadcrumbs as we venture into Judy's wardrobes.'

The light–hearted banter soothed the awkwardness of the date or no date issue.

'Gordon said to give you these for Jock to let him try out his new milk chocolate truffles.' Euan handed them to Judy.

'Tell Gordon thanks,' she said.

The ladies picked up their bags, put their cardigans and jackets on, settled their tab with Gordon and started to head out.

Poppy bid the ladies goodnight.

'Hang on a minute and I'll walk you back to the cottage,' Euan offered, throwing his chef whites off and running into the kitchen to grab his jacket.

'I can find my own way to the cottage, Euan,' she called to him.

Minnie nudged Poppy. 'Let him walk you home. He's a trustworthy type, and although it's safe around here, it's dark in the fields and you're not sure of your surroundings yet.'

Poppy thought this was sensible, and she did want a chance to talk to Euan.

Euan threw his jacket on and hurried back through to Poppy.

'Remember your cake,' Gordon hissed at him.

'I'll just pick something up,' Euan told Poppy. 'Be with you in a minute.'

Poppy smiled to herself seeing Euan in a tizzy.

The ladies filtered away in all directions, and Poppy stood for a moment outside the tea shop gazing out at the sea and breathing in the night air.

Euan emerged with two bags and handed one to Poppy. 'Gordon has put a big slice of your chocolate cake in there and some truffles.' He didn't tell her about the Victoria sponge that was in a cake box in the other bag. Gordon had packed it so that it wouldn't get squished. Euan carried it carefully as they headed off down the esplanade and up the narrow road that led to the fields.

'Thank you for asking me to go to the party night,' Poppy said as they walked together. He towered over her, but she was sure she saw his shoulders slump when she added, 'I want to clarify something about going with you to the party...'

Euan sensed what was coming. She didn't want it to be a date. She wasn't interested in him romantically. She just wanted to keep things light and friendly. Just friends with her new landlord.

'I know what I said in the tea shop,' she continued. 'But I wanted to emphasise privately that I'm not planning to date anyone for the foreseeable future. I'm not suggesting that you're interested in dating me, but I just need to let you know how I feel at the moment about becoming romantically involved.'

'You made it quite clear earlier,' he said, hoping he didn't sound cut to the bone. 'And I'm not thinking of dating either, not with all the work I have and the busy seasons coming up.'

'So, we're clear?' she said.

'We are.' He forced a smile.

They continued to walk further along the road and into the fields.

Poppy gazed up at the deep blue sky arching over the landscape. 'I can see the stars. The sky is so beautiful here.'

'It is. I wouldn't want to live anywhere else.'

'I hope that the temporary six month lease on the cottage is something I'll want to extend.'

'I hope so too.' He was tempted to tell her that he didn't want or need a limit on the lease, but he kept his comment to himself.

CHAPTER FIVE

Euan didn't linger when they reached the cottage.

He bid Poppy goodnight, standing in the garden, making sure she'd remembered her key and that she was home safely.

He waved casually and walked away.

Poppy watched the tall figure merge with the shadowed night and disappear into the nearby fields that led to his farmhouse. She sensed she'd upset him, or worse, upset herself and tilted the balance of what might have been between them.

She stood in the open doorway, lit by the glow of the hallway lamp, feeling the sudden chill in the sea air. The scent of the garden's flowers still lingered in the air and she noticed that there were fragrant night scented stock flowers growing near the rose tree — flowers she intended including in her new designs. Unsettled, she decided to get her sketch pad and draw the night scented stock flowers. They were at their finest in the evenings.

The light from the hallway illuminated the garden and the silvery glow from the sea reflected across the fields. She snapped a couple of pictures of the flowers with her phone and then sketched them, an easy outline of the pale lilac petals and the shape of the leaves was all she needed.

Casting a glance in Euan's direction, she saw the windows of his farmhouse were now aglow. He was home, as was she.

Taking her sketch pad, she went inside and closed the cottage door to the world.

The unsettled feeling disturbed her sleep, and in the depths of the night she got up from the comfy bed and padded through to the kitchen for a glass of milk.

The bag with the chocolate cake was sitting on the kitchen table where she'd left it. She tucked it into one of the cake tins and sipped her milk while looking out the window at the back garden. Tiny solar lights were entwined at the far end of the garden, subtle illumination, reminding her of fireflies flitting through the greenery, lighting up the darkness.

What a beautiful cottage and garden she was living in. She couldn't let her feelings for Euan take the shine off this.

Flicking the kitchen light off, she wandered back through to the bedroom, climbed under the pretty patchwork quilt and gazed out at the night sky. She had a view of the front garden. Yes, this was perfect she told herself. In the morning she'd set up her embroidery and start work on her designs.

Euan lay awake in bed. He couldn't stop thinking about Poppy. Somehow, he had to curtail his hopes of dating her, to avoid the bitterness of disappointment, and to adhere to her wishes. She'd made it abundantly clear that she didn't want to get involved with him. He would not compromise her in any way. He didn't want her to feel uncomfortable around him.

He planned to deliver the desk and table in the morning, and then let her get on with her work. An unobtrusive landlord. Of course, he'd give her the cake too. And then be done with any more nonsense and lies.

Unaware that Poppy's world was in flux due to moving to the cottage, customers had continued to buy her embroidery patterns, downloading them from her website. Several regular customers also wanted to buy her new kits.

Poppy quickly read through her emails after having showered and dressed. She'd even succumbed to a bowl of porridge, something she hadn't eaten in years, but Euan had put the notion in her mind and she relished the hearty breakfast.

The beep of a horn startled her and she gazed out the living room window to see a van pull up outside.

Euan jumped from the driver's side and one of his farmhands, a fit looking young lad, opened the rear doors and started to unload the furniture.

Euan saw Poppy at the window and waved to her. She hurried outside.

'This is the table I had in mind for the spare bedroom. What do you think? I'll take it back if it's unsuitable,' said Euan.

'No, it's perfect.' It was sturdy yet stylish. Ideal for her cutting and packing.

She led the way as Euan and the lad took an end each and carried it inside. They sat it down in the middle of the room, then went back outside for the writing desk. Poppy followed them, eager to see it.

The polished veneer shone in the pale sunlight and she smiled at Euan. 'It's beautiful.'

Euan nodded to the lad and they carried it into the living room.

'Where would you like it set up?' Euan asked her.

'Over there at the wall between the window and the fireplace.' She'd already planned where she'd put it. There was a table near the window where she wanted to sit and embroider using the natural light shining in. The desk would still receive plenty of light, but also benefit from being near enough to the fire to feel cosy when she was working on her art and designs.

'I brought a couple of chairs,' said Euan. 'I thought you may want one of them. They're old fashioned but comfortable and an ideal height for the writing desk and the table.'

Poppy went with him to view the chairs that were in the back of the van.

Euan reached down and offered her his hand. 'Jump in and try them for size.'

She took his hand and he pulled her up with ease.

He pointed to one of the chairs. 'This is the type that I have in my study. They're great for keeping your back straight. I prefer traditional four–legged chairs like this rather than the modern whirly ones.'

Poppy tried it for size. 'This is ideal, and I try to keep my posture in mind when sewing, so I'll take this, thank you.'

He motioned to the other chair. She tried it too and liked it.

'They've both got cushions that go with them.' He'd packed them in the van. He shrugged. 'It's up to you if you want them.'

Poppy wanted everything, mentally planning how great a set up these would be for her work.

The chairs were taken inside and then Euan got ready to leave. 'I won't interrupt your day any longer,' he said and headed outside. 'But I do have one more thing for you.'

The lad had jumped into the passenger seat while Euan reached in and brought out the cake box. He handed it to her. 'One Victoria sponge cake, as promised.'

She opened the box and smiled when she saw it. 'It looks delicious.'

'I baked this myself.' This was true. He had. 'I opted for raspberry jam with the buttercream filling.'

'I appreciate this. What a treat,' she said smiling at him.

His heart melted just looking at her. Whatever the chaos and trouble his promise had caused, the end result was worth it. Poppy was clearly delighted with the cake.

'Right, I'm off. A busy day, as I'm sure you have too,' Euan said brightly.

'Thank you again for the furniture, Euan — and the cake.'

He nodded acknowledgement of her appreciation, jumped in the van and drove off with a cheery wave.

Poppy blinked, thinking perhaps she'd misjudged Euan's intentions. He could've lingered when delivering the furniture, tried to wangle a cup of tea and share the cake. But no, he didn't, and seemed quite happy that she liked what he'd brought.

Taking the tasty cake inside, she put the kettle on for tea, eager to have a slice of the treat he'd baked for her.

While the kettle boiled, she set up the writing desk with her lightbox to begin inking the finished artwork for some of her new designs, and tracing the patterns on to fabric ready for embroidering.

The desk was ideal for this sort of work, and the dookits held the pencils and the pens she used for sketching and inking the illustrations.

When the tea was poured, she cut a slice of cake, opened the kitchen door and let the garden air waft in while she tasted the Victoria sponge. It was scrumptious, and the raspberry jam with the sweet buttercream was the perfect combination. The cake was light and delicious. She was definitely impressed with Euan's baking prowess and with Euan himself. Her heart fluttered thinking about him, and she forced herself not to go tumbling down the romantic rabbit hole. No, thoughts of how strong, capable, thoughtful and handsome he was would only lead to a broken heart. But she could be friends with him without becoming involved.

Mid morning she set up her white cotton and linen fabric for cutting on the table in the spare room and made up several kits for the online orders. The kits included fabric cut to the required size along with the thread and the pattern. Minnie had told her that a courier collected the local craft orders at the post office around teatime.

More online sales filtered through during the day, mainly downloads of the patterns. Customers were also eager to know when they could download and print the new patterns she'd been mentioning in the news updates on her website. She added several new designs including two of the blue florals and a blue butterfly. They included the pattern template, detailed sewing instructions, the stitches and threads used, pictures of the embroidery being worked and of the finished design.

Snatching a cheese sandwich and another slice of Euan's cake kept her going until the afternoon.

Feeling that she'd settled in quite well and had made progress with the orders and the artwork, she sipped a cup of tea and wandered out into the front garden for a breath of fresh air. The sun had quite a bit of warmth in it, and an abundant selection of flowers were thriving in the garden. She noticed the love–in–a–mist and Cupid's dart flowers, more blue blooms for her designs.

She sat outside on the grass and sketched the flowers while they were at their finest. They would surely fade as autumn replaced the summer. She snapped photos of various parts of the garden to use when the weather changed so she'd have a catalogue of flowers as reference for the illustrations. She wished she'd had the courage and ability to move to a cottage by the sea years ago. What a wonderful way to live.

She'd almost finished sketching when there was a chill in the air and the sea breeze picked up pace.

Spits of rain hit off her sketch paper, and she gazed up at the fast moving clouds that shielded the bright sunlight and shaded the day to a pale grey. The scent of the flowers increased, a sure sign of rain.

She grabbed her artwork and hurried inside, feeling the sense of cosiness that the cottage provided.

Snuggling into a comfy chair in the living room, she continued to work while listening to the soothing sound of the rain hitting off the windows. She felt safe from the world, and excited too. She wasn't sure why, just a sense of potential in the air.

Euan was used to working in the rain. Heavy downpours and storms could lay waste to some flowers, but most weren't so fragile that they didn't benefit from a wee bit of drizzle or a thirst quenching shower.

Rain ran down the back and shoulders of his waxed jacket as he worked in one of the fields, checking the progress of the crops. They were doing nicely. The earthy scent of the land mingling with the lush greenery was invigorating. He breathed it in, working hard, feeling the tasks keep his muscles lean and strong.

He'd told himself that he wouldn't keep looking over at Poppy's cottage, but as the rain dripped off his uncovered hair, running rivulets down his handsome features, he blinked to clear his view and saw nothing except the cottage itself in soft focus. Poppy would be inside, cosy, working away. He hoped she enjoyed the cake.

The rain didn't last long, and by mid afternoon the sun glinted off the flowers and leaves in the cottage garden, everything refreshed, including Poppy. Cocooned in the cottage without the stress of the city pressing down on her was so relaxing even when she'd been inking her artwork. The finished artwork took quite a bit of skill and concentration to create the designs for the embroidery templates. The sound of the rain soothed her senses and she now felt as fresh as the garden appeared to be.

She put on a pair of boots that she wore for trekking through the city on rainy days and stepped outside. Breathing in the air felt like a dose of nature's aromatherapy. The scent of the flowers, fields and sea mingled in the sunlight.

She squinted at the sea that was visible from the cottage garden, shielding her eyes from the brilliance of the glare. Again, she told herself she'd done the right thing coming here, even more determined to make her embroidery business thrive.

Her packages were all set for posting, so she put them in a bag and ventured down to the esplanade, handed them into the post office for collection by the courier, and then headed to Minnie's shop.

Poppy picked up some groceries while Minnie served a customer. The shop was well stocked with everything she needed, including a selection of vegetables fresh from the fields in the local area. A bag of potatoes, carrots, onion and a cabbage were her first choices, then she added salad items, tomato sauce, a jar of pickle, a crusty farmhouse loaf and milk.

Minnie nodded her acknowledgement to Poppy while she finished serving the customer and then gave Poppy a welcoming smile. 'How are you settling into the cottage? Did you get a great night's sleep? On your own, not with Euan, I wasn't hinting at that.'

Poppy giggled as Minnie continued. 'Did he walk you home as promised? He seemed to be all in a tizzy last night.'

'Euan walked me home, nothing more.' Poppy put her groceries on the counter, and that's when she noticed the dog sleeping in his basket.

'That's Bracken. He's tuckered out from galloping along the sand.'

'He's a cutie.'

'He is, and great company for me.'

'Are you on your own, Minnie?'

'I am, sort of, well...' she smiled and confided. 'I was married for years and when I lost my husband, I'd no intention of getting involved with another man. I was settled with my shop, with the quilting bee.'

'But...?' Poppy encouraged her, sensing a secret was about to be revealed.

'Shawn, a big, strapping farmer has been making a play for me these past months, and sometimes...I've been inclined to succumb. Nothing raucous or scandalous.'

'No, of course not.' Poppy sounded unconvinced.

And then they both burst out laughing.

'Men!' Minnie huffed. 'The trouble they get us girls into. You'll know all about that with Euan circling you like a lovestruck lad.

'We've agreed to keep things on a friends only basis.'

Minnie guffawed.

Poppy blinked.

'Sorry, but when you have to decide to be friends because you fancy the nancies off of each other, it's a road that leads to all sorts of mischief and misunderstandings.'

'Minnie!' Poppy exclaimed.

'Och, you know what I mean.'

Poppy smiled and nodded. She knew exactly what Minnie meant.

'I've no plans to complicate things when I've only just arrived,' said Poppy.

45

'I don't want to burst your bubble, but you've a snowball's chance in a frying pan of doing that. Life here is fast–paced in a tranquil setting. It's like we all buzz around in the lull of the landscape while causing equal measures of mayhem and happiness. We're like the tides on the shore. The tides goes out smooth and then comes back with a frothy load of bubbling trouble. Many a person who has moved here from the city for a quiet life is taken aback by the liveliness of our wee community.'

'Including dating a big, strapping farmer?' Poppy teased her.

'Who is dating a big, strapping farmer?' a man's voice boomed as he strode in, filling the shop with his height and broad shoulders.

Minnie's eyes widened and the guilt showed on her face.

Realising this must be Shawn, Poppy threw herself under the guilty bus. 'Minnie was advising me not to date someone that might have a fancy for me. Maybe, possibly, sort of.'

'If you say so,' Shawn said with a disbelieving grin. A sexy grin, Poppy noted, understanding why Minnie had succumbed to being tempted by this strong, fit and mature farmer.

'Poppy was referring to Euan,' Minnie told him.

Poppy glared at Minnie, but the comment was out, and Shawn reversed his opinion.

'Oh, so Euan's chasing your tail, is he?' he said to Poppy.

'He baked her a cake,' said Minnie.

'Romantic rather than raunchy,' Shawn assessed. 'I can be the romantic type too.' He'd brought a long stem wildflower picked from a field and handed it to Minnie. 'I saw it on passing this way and thought of you.' He handed Minnie the flower, gave her a smacker of a kiss on the cheek and then headed out with as much bluster as he'd entered.

'He seems like a handful,' said Poppy.

Minnie twirled the wildflower in her hands, and her cheeks burned pink. 'Oh, yes.'

'Is he hinting that you're a wee bit wild, Minnie?' Poppy teased her.

Minnie straightened her lilac cardigan that was buttoned up over her blouse. 'He can hint all he wants, but I can assure you I'm more of a shrinking violet.'

They were still laughing when Judy walked in. 'I thought I saw you come in here,' she said to Poppy. 'Would you like to have a peek at the dresses for the party?'

'Yes, that would be great,' said Poppy. She paid for her shopping, smirked at Minnie, and then walked along to the bar restaurant with Judy.

CHAPTER SIX

'Minnie looked flushed,' Judy commented.

'Shawn came in to kiss her and gave her a wildflower.'

'I think he's considering asking her to marry him.'

'She should, shouldn't she?'

Judy shrugged. 'Maybe, but Minnie's set in her ways. Perhaps she could have the best of both, her freedom and hot dates with Shawn.'

'It would be quite an unsettled life,' Poppy reasoned.

'But exciting.' Judy sighed. 'I've been lucky in love. I met and married Jock. He's a tiger in bed, a lion in business, and a big softie when it comes to helping people. I love him to bits. I always have, always will.'

They smiled and were still chatting about dating handsome men as they walked into the bar restaurant.

'Here comes trouble,' Jock said by way of introduction.

'No trouble from us, Jock,' Judy told him.

'There's always trouble with you, Judy. And I see you've brought an accomplice.' He stepped forward and extended his hand. 'I'm Jock, Judy's husband, though you probably know more about me that I do about you. Am I right in thinking you're Poppy, the young lass that has Euan's boxers in a twist?'

'Jock!' Judy scolded him.

But the way it was said, and Jock's manner, made Poppy laugh and feel welcome. These people were more open about their feelings than what she was used to. But she preferred their openness to the fake smiles and people talking behind her back that she'd become accustomed to in the office. The comments about her dating the boss had been awful. Leaving that company was one of the best moves she'd made.

Judy led the way upstairs. 'Poppy and I are going dress hunting.'

'I'll see the two of you tomorrow then?' he joked.

'I'll be down to help with the bar fairly soon,' Judy told him. 'Oh and, Poppy's an expert at ceilidh dancing.'

Jock was taken aback. 'Are you pulling my sporran, Judy?'

'No, no joking. She even considered competing. So you'd better have your kilt pleats in order to compete with this young lady.'

They left Jock flabbergasted and hurried on up the stairs into the bedroom that was dominated by wardrobes full of dresses.

'You weren't kidding,' said Poppy. 'I've been in fashion boutiques that have less stock on the rails.'

'I never joke when it comes to dresses. They are my passion. Second only to Jock.'

Poppy smiled. 'I'm spoiled for choice.' Her eyes skimmed the colours, the fabrics, the different styles from traditional tartan, fifties full skirts, cocktail numbers and classic designs.'

'You go and help Jock,' said Poppy. 'I'll see both of you tomorrow.'

Judy laughed. 'You like what you see?'

'I love everything.'

'Okay, let's start by narrowing it down. Do you want a tartan dress or something less traditional?'

'I love that blue dress.' She pointed to a lovely sky blue dress.

Judy reached in and unhooked it from the rail. She laid it on the bed. 'One down, loads of others to go...'

A while later Poppy stood in front of the full length mirror, sweeping her hands down the silky fabric of the blue dress.

'I think you nailed it first time,' said Judy, 'but these are close seconds.' She held up a pale lemon dress that had a full skirt, and a hot little red number with sequins and chiffon.

Poppy sighed. 'What do you think?'

Judy popped the lemon and the red dress in a bag and checked that the blue dress fitted perfectly. 'I think you should go with the blue, and the yellow and the red.'

'I can't possibly borrow three dresses.'

'Of course you can. By the time the ceilidh's over, I'll have replaced at least one of them. I've almost finished sewing this dress.' She pointed to a sewing machine tucked into the corner. Beside it was a half finished rose print tea dress.

Poppy changed back into her jeans and top.

Judy added the blue dress to the bag. 'Take them and live with them for a couple of days. Try them on in your cottage with accessories, the right shoes — you do have shoes you can dance in?'

'I do.'

'Fine, see what one makes you feel gorgeous and deserves to be worn at the party. And take into account the dancing. You being a dancer should know what I mean.'

Poppy nodded, accepted the bag and gave Judy a hug. 'You're so kind. Thank you. I'm really looking forward to the party night.'

'Still going as Euan's date?'

'As friends.'

Judy nodded and didn't comment.

Ceilidh music sounded from downstairs.

Judy smiled. 'I hear the sounds of a man excited to have a great dancer in our midst.'

'He doesn't expect me to dance before I leave, does he?'

Judy shrugged. 'You could make a run for it out the front door, but fair warning, Jock's a fast runner and he'll be after you to see if your steps are up to scratch.'

Poppy didn't mind, in fact, when they went downstairs and she saw the dance floor in the function room at the back of the bar restaurant, her heart rate increased with excitement. The urge to take to the dance floor, something she used to love, but hadn't done in ages, took her back to the past when she danced for the love of it.

'I know you're a busy young woman, Poppy, but can I tempt you to have a wee burl before you go?' said Jock. He'd changed into his kilt and smiled at her. A strong and sturdy man, he suited wearing it.

Throwing all excuses and inhibitions aside, Poppy put her bags down and walked on to the dance floor. She wore flat shoes with her jeans that were soft and pliable and ideal for the dance she was about to do. She recognised the music for the dance that Jock had in mind.

Judy smiled, delighted that Poppy had the heart to do this. Many a young woman in her circumstances would've bolted, blushing, making an excuse to leave. But not Poppy.

Turning up the volume, Jock bowed. Poppy curtsied, and then the two of them let rip across the dance floor, whirling, burling, linking arms, doing the tricky footwork, timing everything well.

The look on Jock's face said it all. Poppy was a better dancer than him, and he didn't mind. This was great. Someone to challenge him. He loved that. He'd always wanted to practice with a top notch dancer. Now here she was.

As the first dance ended, Judy applauded and cheered. Jock held his hand above the sound system. 'One more wee dance before you go, Poppy?'

'How about a reel?' she suggested. 'For the three of us.'

Judy was happy to join in, and the customers in the bar restaurant were treated to a lively display before Poppy headed back along the esplanade. The sea breeze was a welcoming refresher, but she was surprised that she wasn't as out of practice with the dancing as she imagined. It had all come back to her, the exhilarating feeling, whirling around the dance floor without a care in the world.

And then she thought about Euan. If his boxers were in a twist at the quilting bee, just wait until the party night dancing.

Smiling to herself, she walked past Gordon's tea shop, aiming to go back to the cottage to prepare a tasty dinner. In the daylight she admired the shop's canopy and noticed that the hanging flower baskets had blue lobelia flowers trailing from them.

'Poppy!' Gordon called to her. 'Want a cuppa? You look like you could do with it.'

She glanced back at him. 'I've been dress borrowing with Judy and ceilidh dancing with Jock,' she explained, taking Gordon up on his kind offer.

'Take a seat,' he said, sitting her down at one of the tables at the window with a view of the sea. Sunlight streamed in the open door along with the breeze. She hung her bags on the back of her chair and relaxed while Gordon served up a pot of tea.

He checked the time. 'It's nearly teatime. Would you like something to eat? It's on me.'

'Are you sure? I don't want to put you to any extra work.'

He nodded and pointed to the sandwich board outside the door. 'Today's special is lentil soup, crusty bread, green salad and a slice of my savoury quiche.'

Everything he offered tempted her. So she said, 'Yes, that would be wonderful.'

Gordon served it up in a flash and sat down for a moment to chat to her.

'This is the tastiest lentil soup I've had,' she said.

'Thank you. It's an old fashioned recipe with extra carrot and onion.'

51

She eyed the savoury quiche. 'This is very welcome. I had porridge for breakfast and then nothing more than a few bites of a sandwich. And cake. Two slices of Euan's home baked cake.'

Gordon smiled and didn't correct her on the home baking. Technically it was baked in the tea shop, but that didn't matter. The taste and success of Euan's efforts had been worthwhile.

Gordon asked her about her embroidery work. 'So you sell your embroidery patterns on your website?'

'Yes, most customers are interested in downloading the patterns so they can start stitching the embroidery right away. Online patterns are my top sellers. I sell kits too, but these require me to cut fabric and thread and include other items depending on which kit they buy, and then package them up for posting.'

Gordon nodded. 'Being able to sell online has been a game changer for the ladies of the quilting bee. Many of them have started up lucrative wee craft businesses. And now they have their quilting bee website too.'

'I've joined that,' Poppy told him.

'What cottage is it that you've moved into? I'm still reasonably new to the area and still learning about all the cottages. I live above the tea shop.'

'The cottage is in the new field that Euan bought, next to his other fields.'

Gordon shrugged still unsure.

Poppy laughed and pointed in the direction of the function room garden. 'Over there. The white cottage with the pink windows and pink door.'

'Ah, I know the one. It's a quaint cottage with a garden set in part of the field.'

'That's the one.'

'Does it have a name?' he asked. 'Most of the cottages have names, even if it's only the bakery cottage.'

Poppy shook her head. 'It doesn't have a name.'

Gordon frowned. 'You'll have to give it a name,' he said, making her realise that he was right. 'If it's going to be your business, it would be part of your marketing.'

She thought about calling it after herself, but that didn't appeal to her. They tried out several variations, names that included pink, cottage and flowers.

52

Then Gordon had a suggestion. 'There's the bakery cottage, so how about the embroidery cottage?'

'Perfect,' Poppy enthused. 'I like that.'

Between Gordon checking on things cooking in the kitchen, and serving a couple of customers, they went on to discuss other aspects of business, his tea shop and how he'd decorated the front with hanging baskets.

'I noticed you have blue lobelia flowers,' she said. 'Would you mind if I took a picture of them for my embroidery designs? I'm including lots of blue flowers and those are so sweet.'

Gordon was happy to oblige. In fact, he took her phone off her as she stood outside, and being as tall as Euan, he reached up and snapped close–ups of the tiny flowers for her.

'There you go,' he said, handing the phone back.

She flicked through the images. 'These are ideal. Thank you.'

Then he remembered about the tea shop's back garden. 'The roses are in full bloom. Beautiful pink roses. Come on through and take a look.'

Poppy followed Gordon out into the garden. He cupped one of the flower heads gently and held it up for her to see. 'Isn't it gorgeous? And it smells so nice.'

The fragrance reminded her of a light scent she used to wear. 'The roses are beautiful.' She snapped pictures of those and a couple of hellebore that were growing near them.

As they headed back through the tea shop for Poppy to be on her way, Gordon paused.

'Do you accept commissions?' he asked.

'Yes, but I've only embroidered a few.'

'I'm always looking for vintage items for the tea shop. A couple of weeks ago I saw embroidered lettering for the words *Tea Shop* in a frame. I made a bid for it, but it went sky high and someone else bought it. It was an original vintage piece of embroidery. But I wondered...do you embroider lettering?'

'I do. Is it the words Tea Shop that you want?'

'Yes, I'd like to frame the embroidery and hang it behind the front counter.'

'What type of lettering style?'

Gordon wasn't sure.

'I could embroider the words in a classic chain stitch using a single colour of thread, or two colours. There are various other stitches that look pretty for lettering — split stitch, stem stitch, whipped back stitch...'

'I'll leave that up to you,' he said. 'I don't know anything about embroidery.'

'Would you like any embellishments on the lettering?'

Gordon shrugged. 'You're the designer. What do you think would look nice?'

'I'll put a design together and show you the pattern before I stitch it,' she suggested. 'I'm sure I can embroider something you'd like. I love embroidering lettering, and I think it would look beautiful framed.'

'Framed seems suitable as it would keep the embroidery clean.'

'I'll design a pattern that can be framed for your tea shop.'

Gordon nodded enthusiastically. 'I'll leave that with you then.'

Both happy with their agreement, Gordon waved Poppy off as she left him to get on with his work. The tea shop was becoming busy with customers arriving for the early evening teatime specials.

Poppy was so busy checking the flower images on her phone, while carrying her bags of shopping and the dresses, that she didn't notice Euan walking towards her. She would've bumped right into him if he hadn't alerted her.

'Hey, there,' he said. 'Been shopping?'

'Shopping, dress borrowing and being fed and feted at Gordon's tea shop,' she told him. 'He's commissioned me to do a tea shop embroidery for him.'

'You've been busy then.'

'Happily so.' She showed him the flower images on her phone. 'These are from the tea shop's hanging baskets and the back garden. Aren't they gorgeous?'

Euan nodded, taking in her lovely features and her open smile as she leaned close to him to show him the pictures on her phone. Almost on tip–toe, she forgot for a moment that she was leaning into him, smiling so close that her lips were a breath away.

'Gorgeous,' he said, though he was referring to Poppy.

Unaware of the fireworks of emotions she was setting off inside him, she stepped back and put the phone in her bag. 'I hope it's okay with you, but I'd like to give the cottage a name.'

54

He nodded. 'Yes, what do you want to call it?'

'Embroidery Cottage,' she said cheerfully. Wide grey eyes waited for his reaction.

'A lovely name,' he said.

Delighted he agreed, she couldn't stop smiling. 'How was your day?'

'Productive.'

Then she gasped, realising she hadn't complimented him on his baking. 'The cake, your cake...it was delicious. I've eaten half of it. It kept me going while I was busy working.'

He smiled broadly. 'I'm pleased you enjoyed it.'

'Now I guess it's my turn to bake a cake for you.' The enthusiasm of the moment made her offer something that if she'd thought it through she wouldn't have done.

'You don't need to,' he said, hoping she would bake him a cake.

'Do you like carrot cake?'

'I love carrot cake. I'm one of Gordon's top customers for a slice of that.'

Poppy smiled up at him. 'Carrot cake it is. I don't have the ingredients at the moment, but I promise I'll bake one soon.'

'No hurry.'

She nodded and smiled. 'Well, I'd better push on. Lots to do.'

'Including trying on dresses?'

'Number one priority.'

He peeked in the bag. 'That blue dress looks pretty from what I can see of it.'

'I love the blue one. I'll probably wear it to the party, but the yellow and the red are hot contenders too.'

'I'm sure you'll look lovely whatever one you select.'

'Judy's wardrobes are full of dresses,' she told him. 'And I ended up ceilidh dancing with Jock before I left the bar restaurant.'

'Did Jock approve of your dancing? He tried to teach me some fancy steps, but I kept burling the wrong way.'

Poppy nodded. 'I'll keep you right. Besides, it's just for fun. No one will be competing against each other.'

'I'll be sure to wear my kilt,' he said. 'No kilt, no ceilidh dancing. Jock's rules.'

'You've got the physique to carry off wearing a kilt.' She bit her lip, wishing she hadn't made such a personal remark.

'I'll take the compliment while it's going,' he said. 'I know we're just going as friends.'

He looked so handsome standing there with the early evening sunlight emphasising his rich golden hair. His hazel eyes appeared more green than tawny, and the way he smiled at her made her heart flutter.

'Friends,' she agreed, hiding her feelings. But it was for the best. It was always for the best. She smiled and started to walk away.

'I didn't realise you did commissions,' he said, his words pulling her back.

'A few.'

'As flowers are one of your specialities, it would seem ideal that you'd embroider some for me, to hang in my study.'

'I'd be happy to do that. The one I'm designing for Gordon is going to be framed and hung up in the tea shop. I assume you'd want yours framed rather than left in the hoop.'

'Framed sounds great.'

'What type of flowers would you like?'

'I like all sorts, but I do love blue flowers and those with autumn tones.'

'Perhaps something like love–in–a–mist, forget–me–nots or sunflowers?'

'Yes, they sound ideal.'

'I'll sketch some samples and run them by you before I start on the embroidery,' she told him.

'Thank you, Poppy.'

'Okay, I'm going to run now,' she said.

He nodded and smiled as she hurried away. In his heart he would keep his promise to be friends only, but every time he encountered her, he wished that things were different.

He watched her slender figure walk away along the esplanade, and then he turned around and continued on his way towards Gordon's tea shop. He hadn't thanked Gordon properly the previous night for teaching him to bake, and wanted to pop in and tell him personally before going back to his farmhouse for dinner. First, he'd promised a customer he'd drop by to discuss an order of flowers for an anniversary event, and headed there to give them a list of flowers they could select from. The man was working on his boat in the harbour and Euan went over to talk to him. Their discussion went on

56

longer than he'd intended, and veered into topics like scraping your barnacles and keeping your cockpit ship shape. When Euan finally finished, he saw that the tea shop looked quite busy.

CHAPTER SEVEN

Gordon was buzzing around serving customers when Euan walked in. Bad timing. Euan had thought that he'd catch him before the tea shop became busy.

Gordon perked up when he saw Euan and waved him through to the kitchen.

'I can see you're busy,' Euan began, 'but I wanted to thank you for teaching me to bake last night. Poppy says she enjoyed the cake and—'

'I don't suppose you've got half an hour to spare?' Gordon asked, nodding acknowledgement of the thanks, but desperate for help.

'Eh, yes—'

'I'm so busy with customers. It must be the mild weather bringing them down to the shore. Would you mind helping out in the kitchen? Just until I catch up. There's extra orders for quiche and salad. Could you cut the quiche into slices and add a salad garnish?'

Euan frowned, catching most of what Gordon wanted him to do.

'Grab a clean apron, and remember to wash your hands,' Gordon instructed him.

Seeing that Gordon really could do with a bit of help, Euan put on an apron, managed to tie it himself, plopped a hat on as it made him feel like a proper chef, washed his hands and then started cutting up a large quiche.

'How many slices should I cut?' Euan asked.

'Ten per quiche. The other quiche are over there,' Gordon said and then hurried out with bowls of soup and baskets brimming with bread.

'Ten,' Euan said to himself, then began cutting the slices. The quiche smelled so savoury and if there was an extra slice left after the customers had been served, he planned to buy it and take it home for his dinner.

The plates were lined up on one of the long kitchen counters. Euan placed a slice on each plate and then used the utensils in the big bowl of mixed salad to scoop a generous garnish on to the sides of the plates. By the time Gordon came back, he'd almost finished.

'Quick work, Euan,' Gordon said, giving him the thumbs up, grabbing a couple of plates and taking them out to the customers.

Euan glanced around wondering what else he could do to be helpful. He'd seen Gordon making the tea and that's something else he was sure he could tackle.

'Do you want me to make the tea?' Euan offered as Gordon came back to pick up more plates of quiche and salad.

'Yes. Pour it into the ceramic pots.' He pointed to the teapots that were set up on another counter.

Feeling useful and actually enjoying himself working in the kitchen, Euan sorted the tea and then took it upon himself to slice up the fruit cake like he'd seen Gordon doing.

'It's very helpful of you,' Gordon told him.

Euan straightened his hat. 'The good guys always wear white hats,' he joked.

Laughing, Gordon hurried out with more orders, grateful for the back–up on an extra busy evening. He was also running late with the quiche cutting because he'd been talking to Eila on the phone. He missed her so much and although he knew the fashion design course was only for a fortnight, he wished she was home with him. Chatting to her, the time got away from him. Usually he was so organised, but with Eila telling him all about her course, what she'd done that day, the time wore on and he hadn't prepared all the dishes for the teatime customers. Then even more customers had turned up than normal and brought on the frenzy in the kitchen. He breathed deeply. Thank goodness for Euan mucking in.

'Here's the bottle of whisky you wanted for your flaming truffles, Gordon,' said Jock, appearing at the kitchen door.

'Thanks, Jock. I'll settle up with you later.'

'Aye, Gordon. Nay fuss, lad.' Jock glanced at the tall chef busy making the tea. 'Oh, it's yourself, Euan. I didn't recognise you with your whites on.'

Euan smiled round at him and nodded. 'Just helping Gordon during the mad rush, then I'm off home, where I should be.'

'Judy said you've been hiding your culinary talents under your bushel. I thought she was havering, but here you are, so I owe her an apology.'

'I was talking to Eila on the phone,' Gordon explained. 'The time got away from me, so Euan's giving me a hand.'

'You seem extra busy,' said Jock. 'Do you want another pair of hands to clear the decks? The bar restaurant's not too chocca the night.'

Gordon's brows raised in pleasant surprise. 'I would, Jock. Thanks. If you're sure it won't make you short staffed.'

'Ach, I'll spare you a wee while and clear the backlog of orders.' He scrubbed his hands, slung on an apron and hat to match Euan, grabbed one of the chits and read it. 'Another bowl of lentil soup and basket of bread coming up.'

'I wondered where you'd gone,' Judy called into the kitchen, seeing Jock sitting in the kitchen with Gordon and Euan, laughing and drinking drams of whisky.

'Euan and myself were just helping Gordon with the suppers — and he was showing us how he makes his whisky truffles,' Jock told her.

Judy pressed her lips together and shook her head. 'It looks like more whisky has gone down your throats than in the truffles.'

Gordon laughed. 'We may have indulged a wee bit.'

Jock held up the half empty bottle of whisky. 'Aye, we may have done, Judy,' he admitted, and then laughed.

'You're a bunch of rascals. Now come on you, the bar's getting busy. I need you to help serve the customers.'

'Here I come.' Jock removed his chef whites and hung them back on the hook. 'Thanks for the natter and the nonsense,' he said to Gordon and Euan.

'Cheers,' Euan joked, holding up a truffle and then popping it in his mouth.

'Thanks again, Jock,' Gordon called after him as Judy took him away. 'Sorry, Judy for waylaying your better half.'

Judy waved cheerily, leaving a feeling that all was well with the world.

'What's going on with Gordon having Euan in his kitchen?' Judy asked Jock as they walked back to their bar restaurant next door.

Jock paused outside the entrance. 'Ach, at the core, I think it's got to do with Euan trying to impress Poppy, and Gordon missing Eila. She's away for two weeks, but it's made Gordon realise he's dragged his heels and should've asked Eila to marry him.'

'They've not been dating that long.'

'No, but she's in *Edinburgh*,' he emphasised.

'Oh, I see. Cairn?' she said, sounding concerned.

'Don't mention that cold, handsome heartbreaker to Gordon. The penny hasn't dropped yet. He hasn't made the connection between Eila being in Edinburgh and in Cairn's territory.'

Judy looked worried. 'It's not long since Cairn headed home to Edinburgh and gave up fighting for Eila. But maybe if Cairn finds out she's there, he'll make a play for her again.'

Jock nodded firmly.

'What can we do?' said Judy.

'Not meddle for a start.'

'But surely if Gordon realised about Cairn, he'd—'

'He'd what? Let the tea shop run itself while he scooted off to Edinburgh? He could jeopardise his business and his relationship with Eila.'

Judy nodded and sighed. 'Edinburgh's a big city. I suppose if Eila's on a fashion course, she'll be too busy studying to go gallivanting around the city. It's a long shot that she'll bump into Cairn.'

'Is it? According to Gordon, after the classes during the day, the designers all go socialising in the evenings. He trusts Eila, but she's a wee beauty. She's bound to have men coming on to her. And fashion design is still in Cairn's world, part of the men's tailoring, so she's in danger of swimming in his shark pool.'

'I have to do something, Jock. I'll phone Eila and let her know how much Gordon's missing her. See if Cairn has be sharking around.'

'Aye, maybe you should,' Jock agreed. 'But not a word to Gordon. He's up to high doh as it is.'

Judy nodded and they went inside their bar restaurant to deal with their own busy night.

'Eila's out socialising in Edinburgh at night after the classes,' Gordon said to Euan as they both worked on making and serving the tea shop suppers. 'I trust her implicitly, but she's sure to have men flirting with her.' Gordon swirled buttercream on his strawberry cupcakes and shook his head. 'I haven't even put a ring on her finger.'

'You're planning to marry, Eila, though, aren't you?'

'Yes, but I should've proposed before she left. But I didn't want to rush things. You know what it's like. Folk would say I was desperate. You're supposed to take your time.'

'I'm the wrong man to give advice about romance and relationships,' Euan said, before going on to offer advice. 'I'm the prime example of what not to do. I always drag my heels, and other men move in and grab the chance to date women I'm interested in. Don't do what I do. Fight for Eila.'

'I can't go driving up to Edinburgh. She'd think I was acting like a jealous boyfriend.'

'You've no need to be jealous unless...' Euan buttoned his lips and poured more tea.

'Unless what? Spit it out.'

'There's no way to sugar the fact that Cairn lives and works in Edinburgh.'

The realisation hit Gordon so hard that he skooshed buttercream on his apron.

Euan grabbed the piping bag out of his hands and sat him down. 'I'm sorry, I just joined the dots. I hadn't thought about Cairn until now.'

'Neither had I.' Gordon sounded gutted.

'I know Cairn's handsome but—'

'He's double handsome!' Gordon shouted.

'Hello there?' A customer called through to them. 'Any chance of a couple of yum yums and a jammy doughnut?'

'Coming right up,' Euan said, smiling.

Gordon was still slumped on a kitchen chair while Euan ran through to serve the cakes from the front counter.

'What one is a yum yum?' Euan asked the customer, poised with his tongs to pick it up.

'The twisty one,' the customer said, pointing to it. 'I thought a chef would know that.'

'Just joking with you,' Euan lied.

After serving the customer at speed, he hurried back through to the kitchen.

'What should I do?' said Gordon.

Euan hadn't a clue. 'What we need is expert advice.'

They both looked at each other and said in unison, 'Minnie!'

'Calm down, Gordon,' Minnie said, listening to him reel off the predicament over the phone. 'Eila's not going to get involved with Cairn. She loves you, not him.'

'Yes, but—'

'I understand you wish you'd put a ring on her finger. But you can tell her she's welcome to have a long engagement, take the pressure off of thinking she has to start buying wedding magazines and selecting a colour scheme for her bridesmaids' dresses.'

Gordon felt a sense of hope wash over him. 'Yes, I could buy her a ring, get engaged and then give her time to decide when she wanted to get married.'

'There's a risk that Eila would want to set a date soon and you'd need to be prepared to push ahead with the wedding plans.'

'I can't think of anything I'd like more.'

Minnie smiled to herself. 'Well then, phone her and bring the conversation round to rings — does she like diamonds or sapphires? Solitaires, trilogy rings or clusters? Yellow gold or white gold?'

Gordon didn't understand what some of those terms were, but he was prepared to take Minnie's word that this would work.

'Okay, I'm going to phone Eila right now,' said Gordon, picturing that she could be out socialising in a bar or club right this minute.

'Let me know what she says,' Minnie told him.

'I will. Thanks for your help, Minnie.' Gordon sounded anxious, hopeful and hyper.

'I'll hold off the customers while you call Eila,' Euan offered.

'Cheers.' Gordon hurried to a corner of the kitchen, took a steadying breath and called her.

Euan checked the orders. Another two customers had ordered quiche. He served up two portions and carried them through to the front of the tea shop.

'Euan!' Poppy gasped, walking in and seeing him busy serving. 'Working another shift at the tea shop?' She'd only popped in to pick up a tea shop menu so she could match the lettering style for the embroidery.

'Gordon's in an emergency pickle,' Euan summarised.

Poppy looked concerned. 'Has something happened?'

'Eila is in jeopardy in Edinburgh. Cairn is in Edinburgh.'

63

Poppy frowned. 'Cairn?'

For a moment Euan forgot that she didn't know anything about Cairn.

'Sholto owns the largest house in this area, high up on the hillside, hidden by the trees. He's rich, powerful and his tailoring business is based in Edinburgh. He rarely comes down to live here, but Sholto and his two sons, Hamish and Fraser, along with his assistant, Cairn, were all here recently.'

'Okay,' said Poppy, 'but is there something I should know about Cairn and these men?'

'They are the most handsome men you've ever seen.'

Poppy smiled.

'I'm not joking. Hamish and Fraser are around the same age as me, as is Cairn. Even Sholto sets the ladies hearts fluttering when he's here.'

'So, Cairn's handsome?'

'Oh, yes, and cold–hearted, but cunningly charming and rich in his own right.' Euan sounded snippy, and Poppy tried not to smile.

'I know you think I'm exaggerating, but ask any woman about Sholto and the others, and they'll tell you the same as me. Cairn made a play for Eila when they were here recently, but luckily she fell for Gordon.'

'If she loves Gordon, what's the problem? If she meets Cairn in Edinburgh, so what?'

'Let me put it this way...Judy loves Jock and they are a secure and happy couple. But he knows fine that even Judy can't help reacting to Cairn and the others. They are in a league of their own and cause ructions for the ladies in this community whenever they're here. Which thankfully isn't often.'

'So it's like having Hollywood heartthrobs visit?'

'Even more handsome. They're top tailors and their suits are immaculate. These men have it all.' Euan paused, realising he was perhaps selling their benefits to Poppy. 'I'm sure you wouldn't like them. They're not your type. They're wily.'

Poppy smiled to herself. Euan's attempt to dissuade her was less than subtle.

'Can I have sprinkles on my cupcake please, Euan?' a customer called over to him.

'You certainly can.' He hurried through to the kitchen and came back with a tub of sprinkles. 'There you go,' he said. 'Lashings of sprinkles.'

'Oooh! Chocolate ones,' the customer enthused. 'I was expecting the plain vanilla.'

'My treat,' Euan said, and then hurried away again to check on Gordon in the kitchen. 'Grab a seat wherever you want, Poppy,' he called back to her. 'I'll be with you in a jiffy.'

She didn't have time to tell him she'd only popped in for a menu.

Euan hurried into the kitchen.

Gordon had morphed back into his cheery self. 'We're engaged!'

'Congratulations.'

'I'd no intention of asking her over the phone, but when I mentioned about the rings, the conversation escalated to me proposing. I'm going to phone Minnie and tell her the news.'

Euan grabbed the half empty bottle of whisky. 'Before you do another thing, you need a toast to your engagement.'

Gordon accepted the dram that Euan poured. They tipped their glasses together.

'To a happy future for you and Eila,' Euan announced.

'Cheers!'

They downed their drams, and Euan realised he felt slightly over watered. 'I feel a wee bit too happy.'

Gordon laughed. 'You've done not bad for a tea jenny, Euan. Though I've had a bit too much whisky myself.'

They were laughing as Poppy called through to them. 'Customers want to see your bonbons, Gordon.'

'Happy to oblige them,' Gordon said and bounded out of the kitchen.

'Did I hear right?' she said to Euan. 'Gordon asked Eila to marry him over the phone?'

'Were you eavesdropping?'

'No, the roars and cheers of you two could be heard down the harbour. The pair of you sound like you've been drinking.'

'Only a sniff,' Euan lied.

'Don't lie,' she said.

Euan showed her the dregs of what was left in the bottle of whisky. 'Jock had some too.'

Poppy giggled. 'Your hat's squinty.'

Euan walked over and stood in front of her. He towered over her, and his eyes twinkled with mischief.

She reached up and straightened his hat. 'There, that's better. You can't have a chef with a squinty hat.'

'I'm not really a chef,' Euan confessed in a whisper, leaning closer to her.

For a moment she thought those firm lips of his were going to kiss her. She'd never know if she would've kissed him or resisted, because the alarm went off in the oven.

'The cakes are ready,' Euan said, moving back smoothly, still gazing seductively at her.

He turned and took the tray out of the oven.

'You look like a chef to me,' Poppy said to him.

Euan pressed his finger to his lips. 'Our secret. I'm just happy that you enjoyed the cake I baked for you.'

In that moment it dawned on her. 'You did this for me?'

His gorgeous eyes gave her an acknowledging look.

'Because I wanted you to bake me a Victoria sponge?' She gasped, rewinding the conversation at the cottage. 'So, you can't bake?'

'I can now.'

'That's the nicest thing any man has done for me in a long time,' she told him.

'You're not angry with me for the little white lies?'

'No, Euan, not at all.' She smiled warmly, filling his heart with hope.

'I don't mean to interrupt your canoodling,' a male customer announced, 'but is there another pot of tea going?'

'We weren't canoodling,' Euan said, hoping to waylay any trouble and gossip for Poppy.

The man grinned and winked. 'Oh, aye, and the moon is made of Scottish cheddar.'

Judy clicked her phone off and hurried to tell Jock the news. He was pouring pints of beer at the bar.

'Gordon and Eila are engaged.'

'That was fast work.'

'Nothing to do with me, Jock. Minnie advised Gordon to phone Eila and talk about diamond engagement rings.'

66

'Subtle, but clearly effective. I guess we've got an engagement party to plan when she comes home.'

Judy beamed with joy. 'I love engagement parties, and weddings.' She then went through to the kitchen to ladle up the soup for the bar suppers.

Jock gazed at her retreating figure thoughtfully. There was something he needed to do.

CHAPTER EIGHT

The first thing Poppy did when she arrived back at the cottage was take photographs of the exterior and the garden in the lingering sunlight. She planned to use these when she updated her website to include her new address at Embroidery Cottage.

She downloaded all the photographs of the new flowers and the cottage on her phone to her computer. Studying the details on the flowers helped her decide how to design the floral patterns.

She started making pencil sketches and then inking some pieces that later she'd trace on to fabric and embroider. All her designs were stitched and adapted until she felt happy with the pattern. Then she'd upload the finished design with pattern instructions for the stitches and thread colours to the website.

As the night drew in, she flicked the lamps on in the living room and worked by the cosy glow, and under the main lamp with its clear light that was perched above the writing desk. The desk was ideal for her design work and the chair was comfy too. She was grateful for Euan giving these to her, and her thoughts kept drifting to Euan even though she tried to fully concentrate on her work.

Two of the floral designs stood out as contenders for Euan's commission — the love–in–a–mist was her favourite choice for him and a forget–me–not pattern she'd been working on. For an autumn coloured flower, she thought that she'd let him see one of her sunflower patterns. He could select what he wanted.

Gordon's tea shop commission was also on her mind, and she was keen to sketch down an idea she had for the lettering. She'd always loved stitching lettering, and the tea shop words weren't too complicated and merited having a couple of tiny teacups and little cupcakes included in the design.

She paused to make a cup of tea and opened the kitchen door to let the evening air waft in. It felt like one of those late summer evenings that had a hint of autumn brewing.

Stepping outside, she gazed at the trees high on the hills that rose up from the coast, and wondered where Sholto's big house was situated. She couldn't see it, but she did see another large house that according to Minnie belonged to a man called Josh. Apparently, he'd been away on numerous business trips recently, popping back occasionally, and was dating a young woman who'd moved from the city to run the bakery cottage. It made her hopeful that she could find happiness here too.

The sound of the kettle boiling drew her back inside and she made a cup of tea. The dinner she'd eaten at the tea shop had been so filling that she still wasn't hungry. The sense of excitement probably had something to do with it too. Excited to be at the cottage.

Taking her tea through to the living room, she sat it down and then thought she'd try on the dresses before continuing with her embroidery work.

She hung the three dresses on the outside of the wardrobe and admired them. The blue was her favourite, but the others were lovely too. She tried on the red dress and stepped into a pair of shoes that had heels suitable for dancing and yet looked stylish with a dress.

There was an old fashioned full length mirror in a corner of the bedroom, and she viewed her image, wondering if the red would be better for the party. She twirled around, feeling how the dress moved and admired how flattering it was, giving her curves when she needed them while emphasising her slender waistline. Judy had a neat figure, and it was handy that they were of a similar dress size, though the three dresses she'd chosen could all be adjusted at the waist with a sash or belt.

Poppy was about to take the dress off and try on the lemon one when there was a knock at the front door.

She peeked out the bedroom window and saw Euan standing there, lit by the lantern hanging outside the front door.

He saw her peer out and nodded to her. He was carrying a large cardboard box. It seemed heavy, and although he wasn't struggling to hold it, she hurried through to open the door.

His face showed his reaction to her wearing the red dress, but he tried to hide his admiration, and indicated about what he'd brought.

'I don't mean to keep disturbing you, Poppy, but I meant to leave you with firewood and kindling. The weather is unpredictable, and the forecast is that we're going to have a cold spell.'

She stepped aside and he carried the box in and strode through to the living room. He put it down beside the unlit fire and then turned to face her. The sparkles in the red fabric shimmered under the lights, and he was clearly taken aback by how gorgeous she looked.

69

'I was trying on the dresses for the party,' she said, admiring him too. He wore a chunky, classic cream jumper, one of those hand knitted patterns with cable stitches that she'd always wanted to try knitting. The style suited him, and under the glow of the lamps his burnished hair had highlights of spun gold.

He ran a nervous hand through the front of his thick, silky, well–cut hair, but a few sexy strands fell back over his forehead, causing her heart to thunder. This man was so sexy. A walking temptation.

They gazed at each other for a moment, and she sensed the attraction between them. He sensed it too, she was sure, but he kept his promise to keep things friendly, and spoke about the fire.

'I see you haven't lit it yet, so that's fine, but this will give you enough to keep a fire burning, and I'll have logs and kindling stocked up in the back garden so you won't run out.'

'I've never had a real log fire before. I'm eager to light it.'

He started to give her tips on lighting the fire with the kindling. All handy tips, and yet...all the while she hoped he didn't realise how her heart pounded just being near him. Perhaps it was the cosy setting of the cottage, but something in her couldn't help how she felt about him. She hid it well though and tried to sound chirpy.

'I appreciate the firewood,' she said, smiling casually, and then she offered him a cup of tea. The offer was out of her mouth before she could curtail it.

'Tea would be great. Milk, no sugar.' He didn't feel over watered now and the earlier effects of the whisky had faded.

While she went through to the kitchen to put the kettle on, he admired her artwork and patterns that were on the writing desk. 'I see you've been busy with your art.'

'The desk is perfect for working,' she called through to him. 'I have my lightbox set up and—'

'Lightbox?' he queried.

She left the kettle to boil and went back through to the living room. 'The thin box that I use for tracing my patterns on to fabric for embroidering. And I use it to ink my final designs for the patterns.'

Euan studied the lightbox. 'Very handy. I'm not artistic. I admire your talent.'

She blushed. 'I've always loved art, sketching, particularly flowers. She stepped closer to show him the ideas she had for his commission. 'These are just rough sketches, but I thought this love–

70

in–a–mist design would look great, and I have forget–me–not patterns and sunflowers.' She showed him the patterns.

'I like all of these. Would it be too much to ask you to embroider them all? Take your time, tend to your business and embroider mine when it suits you.'

'Okay, I'll do that, if you're sure you want them all.'

'I certainly do. These would look great framed in my study.'

'What's the colour scheme of your study? Is it dark wood, traditional, or light and airy. It would help me decide on the thread tones for the embroidery.'

'My study is traditional, so quite a bit of dark wood. My desk is solid oak and the wooden flooring is dark, but there's plenty of light shining in through the windows. In the evenings, I have the lamps on, and I suppose you would call it masculine cosy.'

This is how she'd pictured it.

'Maybe it would be better if you popped over and had a look,' he said.

She did want to nosey at Euan's farmhouse. 'Yes, I could do that.'

'Drop by when it suits you. My door's always open.' He hoped his invitation didn't sound too heavy or hinted that he'd like to be more than just friends with Poppy.

She smiled brightly, and he felt relieved that she hadn't taken his invitation as a ruse to compromise her.

The kettle clicked off and she went through to make the tea.

'Can I have a look at your artwork?' he said. 'I won't disturb anything.'

'Yes, I'm not precious with my work.'

He liked her attitude, but was careful when handling her sketch pad and was peering at the flower photos on her laptop when she carried the tea through on a tray. She sat it down on the table in front of the fireplace.

She'd cut two slices of the cake he'd baked. 'I thought we should eat this so it doesn't go to waste.' She eyed him and smirked.

'I'm really sorry for all the nonsense at the tea shop,' he said, and then confessed to the fiasco of his attempt at home baking.

Poppy laughed. 'No more baking for you, Euan.'

'That's the thing...working with Gordon has been fun. I've become quite taken with baking and the tea shop kitchen is a challenge I've enjoyed. Though I didn't think so when I first started. I couldn't even sift flour or whip up buttercream.'

'Perhaps you should bake the carrot cake,' she suggested jokingly.

'No,' he protested. 'The carrot cake is way above my skill ability.'

She smiled, and he realised she was teasing him.

They had tea and cake, and then she showed him the table that was set up in the small room.

'The table is perfect for my cutting and packing,' she told him.

Piles of her embroideries, fabric and boxes of threads were stashed on the dresser and the table. Her stranded cotton thread selection was divided into main colours — blues, pinks, yellows, greens... Most were kept on the skeins but some were wound around thread cards, labelled and numbered with the exact colours.

He peered in one of the boxes. 'That's a lot of thread.' He lifted up one skein and couldn't imagine how she'd unwind it. He put it back where he got it.

'That's just some of the cotton thread.' She pointed to other boxes. 'Those are filled with crewel wool.'

'You embroider with wool? Like tapestry?'

She shook her head. 'The crewel wool I use is thicker than the stranded cotton and gives a rich texture to an embroidery. It's thinner than tapestry wool, and ordinary knitting wool like double knit yarn.'

Euan smiled. 'You lost me at the stranded cotton.'

'Basically, yes, I use a lot of thread. I can spend hours just organising the colours.'

'I'm like that when it comes to my flowers. A subtle shade difference in the petals catches my eye and I find myself wanting to cultivate new varieties of the same flowers.'

A box of sparkling gold thread caught his attention.

'Those are metallic effect threads.' She moved the skeins and spools aside to show him the layers of silver, green, pink and other shimmering colours underneath. 'I love a bit of sparkle.'

He glanced at the hint of glitter in her red dress. 'Is that the same type of thread?'

Without thinking, she lifted up the hem of her dress and held the fabric under the main light for him to see. 'They're similar, and you can see what a wonderful effect a few strands of metallic can create.'

72

Nothing compared to the effect Poppy was having on him, unintentionally sending his pulse rocketing. She hadn't flashed anything she shouldn't have, but the closeness set his senses alight, and he was glad when she headed back through to the living room.

He breathed, calming himself down, but before he became too relaxed, Poppy showed him how she embroidered her patterns. Euan was interested to see her work.

He lit the fire as the night started to feel colder.

She heard the wind whip across the coast and went over to the window. 'I think the forecast is right. Look at the waves on the sea. They look quite wild.'

He stood beside her at the window, feeling at home with her, comfortable and yet yearning to take her in his arms and say let's forget about being just friends. He wanted to sweep her silky hair aside, kiss her neck and those soft lips of hers. Those sweet lips that kept smiling at him. There was no hint of game playing from Poppy. But an open nature like hers, a warm heart, could so easily be broken. He didn't want to be the man responsible for causing her distress, so he kept a firm grip of his feelings, and tried to be the man she needed him to be — a friend she could trust.

Their laughter filled the living room as she let Euan try his hand at sketching and using the lightbox for tracing.

'Mine look like chicken scratchings compared to your designs,' he admitted.

She tried not to laugh. 'I think you should stick to baking.'

'Huh! My artistic endeavours aren't that bad, are they?'

'You want me to lie?' she said.

'No, I've done enough lying for both of us.'

'Here,' she said, handing him a small embroidery in a five inch hoop. 'Try a few stitches on this cornflower.'

He held his hands up. 'I can't sew.'

'I'll show you.' She placed the hoop in his hands and then instructed him on the sewing. 'Bring the needle up through the back of the fabric, yes, that's right, follow the lines on the pattern, and then take the needle back down.'

He attempted a couple of stitches. 'There are a lot of stitches in this cornflower. What type of stitch is this?'

'Satin stitch. It creates are lovely smooth effect for the petals.'

'It's tricky. Your stitches look perfect.' He tried to keep his in line with the pattern.

'It takes practice, especially for satin stitch, but now you can say you've attempted embroidery as well as baking.'

'This needle is very fine,' he remarked.

'It's a number ten with an elongated eye.'

He handed the embroidery in the hoop back to her. 'My slightly wonky contribution to your pattern.'

'Your stitches aren't wonky at all. I'm keeping them in.'

'What do you do with the embroidery once it's finished?'

'I photograph it and put the pictures on the website to show what the finished embroidery looks like. Then I tuck it away for safe keeping.'

'You don't sell them?'

'No, not those designs if they become a pattern. I keep the original embroidery.'

He found her work interesting. 'How long does it take to embroider something like these cornflowers?'

'I could finish this in a day, probably less. I've been embroidering for years, and I stitch quite quickly. But something like this thread painted bee design with all the flowers in the garland would take much longer. A cottage design takes me two days. It depends on the style of the pattern too. Some are thread painted and others are filled with satin stitch or lazy daisy stitches. Tiny flowers like these forget–me–nots are lazy daisy stitches with a French knot in the centre. They stitch up quite quickly. I find embroidering so relaxing, so I don't bother about the time, unless it's a specific commission or the demand for a new floral pattern on my website.'

He admired one of her blue butterfly designs. 'I love how you've embroidered the wings. Is this thread painted?'

'Yes.' She explained about the thread painting, and agreed that at least one of his pieces would be embroidered with the long and short stitch technique.

He tried his hand at embroidering lazy daisy stitches and couldn't stitch for laughing as he got himself tangled in the thread.

'I don't think lazy daisy is your thing,' she said. 'But you have to attempt French knots.'

More tangled threads and laughter erupted in the living room. There were moments when her soft hands brushed against his strong

74

fingers sending sparks of excitement through her. She blamed her blushes on the heat from the fire.

As they continued to enjoy each other's company, the cottage clock struck midnight.

'Midnight,' Poppy exclaimed. 'It can't be.'

'Time flies when you're having fun and I'm being ridiculed,' he joked. He stood up and got ready to leave.

'Remember to put the fireguard up if you go to bed and the fire's still burning,' he told her.

'I will.'

She saw him to the front door. A storm was brewing. The cold air blew in and she folded her arms across her chest for futile warmth.

'As nice as that dress is, Poppy, I think this is a night for cosy jim–jams.'

She smiled at him, wondering if that's what he wore. She pictured him as more of a boxer shorts and bare chest man in bed. And then scolded herself as she pictured what his lean muscled torso would look like, and feel like to snuggle into.

Thankfully, he'd no idea what she was thinking about him as she waved him off and watched him disappear again into the shadows of the fields. She'd definitely take him up on his offer to drop by his farmhouse. Maybe tomorrow, or would that be too soon? It wasn't long until the party night, and she wanted a peek at Euan's world before she went with him to the ceilidh.

Euan lay in bed trying not think about Poppy and how lovely she looked in her red dress. He'd enjoyed his evening with her, but seeing how hard she was trying to make her embroidery business work, he didn't want to risk ruining everything for her. If he started dating her, he knew his feelings for her were strong. Poppy was the type of woman he dreamed of marrying and settling down with. He hadn't felt like this before, so he knew the strength of his intentions. But what if things went wrong between them as so often happens when it comes to romance? Would Poppy feel she couldn't live in the cottage and move back to the city? The cost to her business, her heart and her hopes would be enormous.

He fluffed his pillow and tried to settle himself. He was always up with the lark every morning. And that would be something else to take into consideration. If they became a couple, would Poppy live here with him at the farmhouse? She loved the cottage and it suited her so well. Another thing he didn't want to ruin for her.

He thumped his pillow into submission and settled down, listening to the sounds of the storm raging out at sea, matching his own inner turmoil.

CHAPTER NINE

Poppy was checking her online orders in the morning when she saw Jock walking up to the cottage.

She went through to the hall and opened the door.

'Morning, Poppy. I wanted to talk to you about your embroidery. In private. I don't want Judy to know.'

'Come on in, Jock.'

'Thanks, lass.'

They went through to the living room.

He pulled out a sheet of folded paper from his jacket pocket. 'I'm no artist, but I wondered if you could embroider something like this for me?' He handed her the paper. 'Gordon said he'd commissioned you to embroider lettering for his tea shop, and I hoped I could commission you to make this for me. I want to give it to Judy as a surprise.'

Poppy looked at the rough sketch. He'd drawn a flowery heart with the names Judy and Jock in the middle.

'What do you think?' he said eagerly.

'I could certainly make a love heart design for you.'

'There's no rush. Whenever you have the time. Embroider whatever wee flowers you think would be nice.'

The flowers were sketchy, as was the shape of the heart, but she got the idea. It wouldn't be difficult.

'I noticed that Judy seems to like tea dresses with rose patterns,' said Poppy.

'Roses are her favourite flower. Pink roses.' Jock sound enthusiastic.

She flicked through her portfolio of designs. Yes, there it was, a rose entwined heart that she'd designed for names to be embroidered in the middle. She showed it to Jock. 'This is one of my heart patterns. Would this do?'

'It's even better than what I had in mind.'

'I could embroider the roses in various shades of pink and stitch the greenery in two shades of green. Pink and green are a lovely combination. I'd embroider your names in a classic style. Nothing too fancy, so that the names are clear.'

Jock nodded. 'Put Judy's name first, then mine. I always put her first.'

'Is this for a special occasion, an anniversary, because I could embroidery the date on it too.'

'No, it's not because of our anniversary or anything like that.' He sighed deeply and then elaborated. 'With all the recent talk of budding romances and engagements, I wanted a wee minding for Judy, to let her know that I still love her as much as the day I married her.'

Poppy smiled at him.

He went on to confide to her. 'Judy and I fell for each other the first time we met. I knew that night when I danced with her that she was the girl for me. We've been best friends and a loving couple for years. She was a beauty when I met her and she's still a beauty.'

Poppy nodded. Judy was very attractive.

'Neither of us are spring chickens, but she's as lovely as ever, while some mornings I feel I look like an auld turkey.'

They laughed, and he continued, 'You'll have heard the name Cairn mentioned recently.'

'Yes. I've heard he's a cold, handsome heartbreaker.'

'Aye, that sums him up. If he comes back, and I'm sure Sholto is planning to come back here fairly soon with his sons and Cairn, all heartbreakers, I'd like them to see this embroidery framed and hung up behind the bar to let them know that Judy is with me.'

Poppy understood. 'I'll make a good job of the embroidery for you, Jock.'

He pressed his finger to his mouth. 'Keep this just between you and me. Don't even hint to Minnie, or the gossipmongers will spoil the surprise.'

'I won't tell anyone,' she promised.

He smiled, knowing he could trust Poppy, and then headed out. 'Let me know the damage. I'm happy to pay extra for your trouble.'

She nodded. She enjoyed embroideries like this, so it would be a pleasure to sew.

Giving her a cheery wave Jock hurried away, keeping an eye out that he hadn't been seen.

Poppy paused for a moment to breathe in the morning air. There were no signs of the previous night's storm, and the garden flowers looked bright and refreshed, but there was a definite change in the air, the scent of autumn, as if the summer had finally faded to make way for the new season.

Poppy went inside, closed the door and cut the white fabric she needed. She traced the heart on and carefully wrote the lettering.

Using a variegated pink thread, she made a start on it, embroidering the roses on the heart with satin stitch, and the stems in green with stem stitch. She planned to sew a bit at a time, between her other work.

She spent the morning embroidering, stopped for a tomato and salad sandwich for lunch, then continued working throughout the afternoon. She loved how the day stretched out here, compared to the fast pace of the city.

After taking her parcels to the post office, she popped into Minnie's shop for fresh milk and groceries.

Minnie smiled at her. 'Are you busy this evening? Would it be okay if a few of the quilting bee ladies, including me, dropped by your cottage?'

'You're welcome to come by tonight,' said Poppy, adding a packet of chocolate biscuits and custard creams to her shopping.

Agreeing that they'd drop by around seven, Poppy paid for her shopping and left Minnie to serve other customers.

On the way back, she headed down on to the sand and walked along part of the shore. The sea looked beautiful and although she wished it was summer and the weather was warmer, she planned to go paddling another day. Swimming? Well, she didn't even have a swimsuit. The perfect excuse for not getting her bahookie chilled in the sea.

Poppy had the tea set up ready for the ladies arriving that night, and lit the fire to make the cottage cosy. She'd made sure that Jock's embroidery was tucked away in a drawer.

The excited chatter of voices alerted Poppy of their approach. Minnie was accompanied by three other members including Pearl. They were laden with their sewing bags and Pearl carried a large cardboard box.

Poppy opened the door and welcomed them into the living room.

Pearl put the box down on the table in front of the fire. 'We brought a welcoming box for you.'

Poppy realised it was like a housewarming party, and felt quite overcome that they'd done this for her.

The contents of the box were unpacked amid the chatter and excitement. Most of the items had been contributed by the members of the quilting bee, but a couple of extras were added from Euan and Gordon.

There were tea lights, a teacup filled with a hand sewn pincushion, a set of knitting needles with a pattern for a bumblebee tea cosy and enough yarn to knit it, padded satin dress hangers, a vintage style polka dot swimsuit from Judy, a box of his chocolates and sweets from Gordon and a set of quilted cushions from Minnie.

'I thought these would be handy,' said Minnie. 'I enjoy making cushions. I hope you like them.'

'I love them. I love everything you've brought me.' Poppy was overcome by their kindness.

Pearl held the last item in a bag. 'Euan had one of the local men, a sign maker, make this for you.'

Poppy gasped when she saw what it was. A pretty wooden sign with the name Embroidery Cottage on it.

'There's a hook outside the front door that you can hang it on,' said Pearl.

Eager to see what it looked like, Poppy hurried outside and hung the little sign up by the chain attachment. She stepped back to admire it, and the other ladies joined her.

'It's official now,' said Poppy. 'Embroidery Cottage.'

The ladies clapped and cheered and then went back inside. They helped Poppy make the tea and cut slices of the large Dundee fruit cake they'd brought with them, glazed with nuts and cherries.

'Have you decided what dress you'll wear to the ceilidh?' Minnie said to Poppy while they stitched the quilts and other items they'd brought with them for an evening's sewing.

Poppy worked on one of the floral embroideries for Euan, with her back propped up comfy with one of Minnie's cushions. 'Not yet. I tried the red one on last night, but then Euan stopped by with firewood so I didn't get a chance to try the others on.'

'I bet that made Euan's night seeing you all dressed up in a little red number,' said Minnie.

Winking and giggling from the ladies made Poppy blush. 'Nothing happened.'

No one was convinced, not even Poppy herself.

Minnie stitched her hexies. 'Did he stay long after he'd dropped off the firewood?'

'He stayed for tea and I showed him my embroidery. The time flew in and before I knew it the clock chimed midnight.'

'Midnight!' Minnie exclaimed.

'Oh yes, Euan's got it bad for you, Poppy,' said Pearl.

Poppy's cheeks flushed, but she joined in the giggling.

The ladies stayed for a couple of hours, and then they all headed home.

Poppy waved them off. She'd thoroughly enjoyed her evening and had managed to get some embroidery done.

Every gift they'd given her was appreciated. She admired the cottage sign, lit by the hanging lantern, and then went in to get ready for bed.

As she got undressed, she decided to try on the lemon dress.

It was lovely, she thought, looking at it in the mirror, but the red dress had more of a wow factor. She then put the blue dress on and couldn't decide if she liked it better than the red. She supposed it depended on the effect she wanted — cool blue or red hot?

Blue was the safer option, one that would suit being just friends with Euan. To wear the red would be playing with fire. She'd been singed by that a few times in the past when dating the wrong men. Not that she had a long list of relationships or fleeting liaisons. Not at all.

She hung the dresses in the wardrobe and got ready for bed.

The delicious aroma of home baking filled Poppy's kitchen. She had the back door open to welcome in the mild morning, and was up early to make a start on Euan's carrot cake and push on with Gordon's tea shop pattern.

While the cake cooled on a baking rack, she scanned in the finished artwork for the design. The lettering was embellished with little flowers and leaves along with tiny teacups, cupcakes, strawberries and cherries to create a modern vintage design. She emailed the design to Gordon so he could look at it when he wasn't busy.

The porridge she'd eaten for breakfast kept her well fuelled while she tackled the online orders. Her new patterns for the autumn were popular. The hard work she'd put into the new flower designs was paying off. The autumn hawkbit flowers, the chocolate cosmos and the acorn borders were selling well. Her patterns included a range of designs — garlands, borders and motifs that could be embroidered and kept in the hoop or framed, stitched along the edges of a tablecloth or cushion, or used as a small motif on an item of clothing.

Poppy finished stitching the roses and greenery on Jock's embroidery. She'd embroider their names on later.

Whipping up the cream cheese icing for the cake, Poppy hoped Euan would like it. She'd bought the ingredients the previous day at Minnie's shop, and used the recipe she'd learned years ago. Carrot cake was one of her favourites, though recently there had been little time to bake, so it felt great to be standing in the cottage kitchen gazing out at the back garden while making the cake.

Euan was working in the field near his farmhouse when he saw Poppy approaching. She was carrying something carefully wrapped in a bag.

He waved to her and she smiled as she walked along a narrow path through the flower field towards the farmhouse.

'One carrot cake as promised,' she announced.

He hurried to take the cake off her, delighted that she'd baked it, but even more pleased to see her. They hadn't seen much of each other since he'd been in her cottage late the other evening. Seeing her chestnut hair shine in the sunlight and her lovely face smiling at him, warmed his heart.

She wore pale grey jeans and a soft pink jumper that enhanced her figure. Her hair was swept back in a ponytail. She'd tied it back to prevent it going in the cake mix. But he loved how it emphasised her pretty features.

'Come in,' he beckoned, leading her into his farmhouse.

'It's a beautiful house, Euan.' She gazed around at the stylish and airy decor. It was a man's home, but she liked the feel of it.

'I'll put this in the kitchen.'

She followed him through, taking in everything from the solid kitchen table that had some of his paperwork on it rather than the remnants of breakfast. If he'd had breakfast, he'd cleared away his dishes. The kitchen was tidy, comfortably so, a family size kitchen with a window overlooking the garden.

Poppy was wearing her pumps, so he hadn't heard her follow right behind him. He was so used to the sound of his own boots on the polished wood floors, and was startled when he spun around after putting the cake down on the table to find Poppy standing in his kitchen.

'Oh,' he gasped, clasping his strong hands on her shoulders to prevent himself from bumping into her. She looked so petite in his kitchen...and quite beautiful.

She smiled up at him and for a moment she felt the connection, the hot attraction between them. She stepped back, hoping to excuse the rising warmth in her cheeks due to the brisk walk across the field.

'I hope I'm not interrupting. I just wanted to hand in the cake,' she said.

'So you can't stay for a cup of tea and a slice of cake with me?' His invitation was clear, and she found herself accepting it even though this hadn't been in her plans.

Euan clicked the kettle on and put plates down on the table. He carefully placed the cake on a large plate and admired it. 'That's better than I'd hoped for. You've been lavish with the cream cheese topping.'

'I always am. If you're going to make a carrot cake, make it luscious.'

Her mouth as she said the word luscious distracted him and he felt the heat in his cheeks competing with hers.

'I'll show you the study while you're here,' he said, walking out of the kitchen, breathing the cool air that was wafting into the hallway. The front door was open and he needed the air to clear his senses. Having Poppy in his house sent his senses for a loop.

He wore an open neck dark denim shirt with the sleeves rolled up to reveal his corded forearms. She reacted to his masculinity in ways she hadn't realised she was capable of. Euan affected her stronger than any man she'd met, or perhaps she wasn't used to this type of outdoors man. His skin still bore the golden tan of the long summer, and those gold highlights in his hair were probably enhanced by the sunlight.

His study summed up Euan, she thought the moment she walked in. There was the antique desk dominating the room, like he'd told her, the dark wood and the light pouring in the windows. His computer was switched on, and she noticed images of flowers on it where he'd been studying new plants for his business.

A bookshelf had lots of reference books on plants, flowers and botanical studies. Some of them looked vintage, original copies, perhaps part of his father and grandfather's collections. She'd read all about Euan on his website, losing a couple of hours going down the rabbit hole into Euan's world, fascinated with his work, and with him. The photographs of him made her heart squeeze. But she felt they hadn't been chosen to flatter him. This was Euan. He was handsome. Whatever the locals said about Cairn being double handsome, she thought that Euan could give him a run for his money in the looks stakes.

'Are you okay?' he asked.

She blinked out of her wayward thoughts. 'Yes, just admiring your study. That's quite a collection of books.'

'All for work, not for leisure,' he said. 'Though as I love my work, I do love reading through these books. Flowers fascinate me. I enjoy reading about the original flower hunters who travelled the world in search of new species.'

'Never fancy setting off to some far flung place yourself?'

'I'm a homebody. Everything I love is right here.' He found himself gazing at Poppy as he realised it now included her.

Sensing the air tingle, Poppy walked over to one of the walls and said, 'The flower embroideries would look nice here. The thread is lightfast so there's no issue with it fading, but the light from the window would show them well.' She stopped herself. 'But where you put your embroideries is your own business.'

'No, I welcome your thoughts,' he insisted.

She suddenly remembered. 'Thank you for the cottage sign. I've hung it up. The ladies brought it along with a welcoming box.'

'I'm glad you like it, Poppy.'

The sound of the kettle clicking off drew them back through to the kitchen.

Euan made the tea while Poppy wandered over to the back door that was partly open. 'It's hard to tell where your garden ends and your field starts.'

'I don't know that it does. Often the field flowers merge with my garden, particularly as the seasons change. When everything is covered in snow it looks like a wonderland.'

'Do you think it will snow later this year?' She hoped it would. She loved the snow but it tended to be fleeting in the city.

'Snow is guaranteed even though we're beside the sea. There's nothing more beautiful than walking along the snowy fields and seeing the sand dazzling white. It snows for at least a month in the depth of winter every year.'

'I'll look forward to that.'

His heart soared, realising that Poppy would be here, months from now, that she'd decided this was the home for her. Bolstered that she wasn't going to change her mind and head back to the city, he washed his hands and cut two slices of the carrot cake.

They sat down at the kitchen table to enjoy it with their tea.

'Gordon's got a strong contender in the carrot cake stakes,' he said, scooping up a mouthful with his fork.

'I'm a home baker. Gordon is in another league.'

Euan pointed his fork at his cake slice and shook his head. 'Nope. They're both delicious in their own way, but I prefer your generous topping. That edges it for me.'

She smiled over at him, and for a moment, she pictured what life would be like if she was involved with Euan. She instantly blinked the thought away, realising that she could make the same mistakes she always did, getting all starry eyed and hopeful, and then having her hopes dashed. She didn't want another dose of that.

...'I've had my kilt cleaned and pressed...'

She realised she'd been so deep in thought that she hadn't been listening properly.

'Have you decided on your dress for the party?'

Poppy smiled brightly and snapped back to concentrate on what he was saying. 'Sort of.' This was the most accurate reply she could give him. In truth, she hadn't decided as she'd been so busy with everything else.

His firm lips curved in a smirk. 'So you're undecided.'

Poppy sighed and nodded. 'I'll probably decide on the night. Throw my clothes off and jump into the dress that takes my fancy.'

Euan's eyes widened.

'Not that I'm saying I run around the cottage starkers.' She blushed, hearing herself make things worse. 'What I mean is, I'll take off all my clothes, jump in the shower and then...'

Euan toyed with his carrot cake, eyes down, but his broad shoulders were shaking with the effort to contain his laughter.

'Laugh,' she chided him. 'Go on.'

'I'm sorry, Poppy, but picturing you running around the cottage in a naked tizzy is...' he started laughing.

So did Poppy. 'Just remember which one of us has two left feet when it comes to ceilidh dancing.'

'I'm sure there is going to be payback.'

Poppy nodded firmly. 'Fierce. So make sure your sporran is tied tight.'

'You're more terrifying than Jock,' he joked.

Poppy smiled wickedly and ate a mouthful of cake.

After they finished their tea and chatter, Euan waved her off.

'I'll see you tomorrow night.' She waved back at him.

'I'm going to enjoy my last day before the utter humiliation on the dance floor,' he called to her.

Poppy laughed, waved again, and didn't correct him.

Euan smiled as he watched her walk away to the cottage, thinking he hadn't enjoyed himself so much in a long time.

CHAPTER TEN

Poppy finished Jock's embroidery in the afternoon. She phoned the bar restaurant.

Judy picked up.

'Is Jock there? I wanted to...ask him about the ceilidh dances.'

'Yes, Poppy, he's right here.' She handed the phone to Jock and continued serving customers at the bar.

'Hello, Poppy,' he said.

'I've finished the embroidery,' she whispered.

'We'll certainly be including all the traditional dances,' he said loudly, so Judy would overhear.

'I'm heading down to the post office with my parcels. Can you meet me outside?'

'I'll do that. See you at the party tomorrow night.' He hung up and smiled casually at Judy. 'Poppy's brushing up on her dances.' Then he checked the time. 'I'm just nipping to the shops.'

None the wiser, Judy smiled as Jock headed out.

Poppy saw Jock further along the esplanade. They walked towards each other, meeting outside the post office.

Poppy slipped the embroidery that was in a bag to Jock. He had a peek. 'It's beautiful.' He smiled with glee, tucked it up his woolly jumper, and glanced around, checking that they weren't being watched.

'It's like one of those spy films where the agents pass secret messages by stealth walking past each other,' Jock whispered.

Poppy smiled and tried to look casual. 'I'm glad you like the embroidery.'

'I'm taking it straight to the framer,' he said. 'I'll settle up with you at the ceilidh.'

'It's a lovely bright afternoon, Jock,' one of his regular customers said to him on passing.

'A grand day for mischief.' Jock wasn't joking, but the man laughed and walked on.

Poppy and Jock gave each other a nod and then went their separate ways. She took her parcels into the post office, while Jock disappeared into a field behind it, heading to the frame maker's house.

Poppy walked along the shore after dropping her parcels off at the post office. The sun created a mellow glow across the sea and there was a stillness in the air. She slipped her shoes off and tested the water. It was cold but soothing, refreshing, so she waded in and continued walking along in the shallows, shielding her eyes from the dazzling sparkles that glinted off the sea.

Maybe one day soon she'd go for a quick swim, especially as there was no excuse because she had the swimsuit that Judy gave her.

After paddling for quite a while, she sat down on the sand and let her feet dry before putting her shoes on and heading back to the cottage.

After having a bowl of tasty vegetable broth for her dinner, Poppy settled down to work on her embroidery. The lights in the living room created a cosy glow, as did the fire.

Gordon had confirmed that he loved the tea shop embroidery design, so she made a start on that, stitching the lettering, embellishing each letter with trailing greenery and ditsy pastel flowers.

The tea shop lettering had a vintage look to it, and the colours of the thread included vanilla, strawberry pink, pale lemon, eau–de–nil and mint green. The design had pale pink teacups, lemon cupcakes, and a couple of little strawberries and cherries added a pop of rich red colour to the pattern.

The fire crackled in the hearth, and out the window she could see the waves across the sea. Stitching the lettering made her want to design lettering for Embroidery Cottage in pretty pinks and floral pastels.

Later, she made tea, put Gordon's embroidery aside, and picked up one of the hoops where she'd been working on Euan's forget–me–nots. She stitched the petals of the flowers and added French knots in the centres.

She thought about Euan as she embroidered the flowers. He'd mentioned that he had his kilt ready. Was she ready to have her heart flutter seeing Euan's fine build wearing a kilt?

Before she could think any more about resisting Euan in his kilt, she heard a text message come through on her phone. Glancing at it, she saw it was from Euan. She read the message: *What type of flowers do you like?*

She frowned and typed her reply. *Flowers?*

Yes, I want to bring some for you when I pick you up for the party. Tradition and all that.

Her heart soared. *Anything would be nice.*

Roses?

I love roses.

Okay, and I'll add a few other blooms to the bouquet.

Bouquet?

A small bouquet. A handful of fresh flowers to celebrate the new season.

Sounds lovely.

He was tempted to say that she was lovely, but kept his fingers in check.

You still there, Euan?

Yes, just making mental notes. And trying not to spoil everything by telling her how much he liked her. *What have you been up to this evening?*

Working on the tea shop lettering, and embroidering your forget–me–nots.

I'm looking forward to having your embroidery hanging up in my study.

I just hope you like them.

He liked her, so he'd like anything she made for him. *I'm sure I'll love them. You have great taste. And speaking of taste, I've scoffed more of that delicious carrot cake you baked for me.*

Better make sure you can still fit into your kilt.

I'll try it on later and adjust the buckles accordingly.

I think you burn up everything due to all the hard work you do. I bet there's a six–pack of lean muscle under your sporran. She pressed the send button and then balked when she read her own message. *What I mean is—*

I'll take the compliment, Poppy. He paused. *Okay, I'd better let you get on with your embroidery.*

What will you be up to?

Adjusting the buckles on my kilt probably.

What colour is it?

My kilt?

Yes, what's the main colours in the tartan?

Blue, deep blues with a hint of light blue. Why?

Just curious. See you tomorrow night.

She went to click her phone off, but another message came through from him.

What are you doing in the morning?

Early morning?

Very early.

Nothing special planned. Having porridge — you've got me started on that. Then getting on with my work. Why?

I heard that you were paddling in the sea.

No secrets in this community.

None. So while the weather is fairly mild, are you up for a quick dip in the sea?

Go swimming?

Yes. I also heard that Judy gifted you a swimsuit, so no excuses about not having a costume.

I know Gordon swims in all seasons, but...

There's only a week or so left when the water won't be freezing cold.

I suppose I should. Okay, I'll do it. I assume you're joining me?

Definitely not, he joked. *The sea is freezing.*

Chicken.

Is that a challenge?

It is.

Challenge accepted. Is your swimming as strong as your dancing skills?

Better, she lied.

I think you're teasing me.

You'll find out in the morning. So test your kilt buckles and give your swimming trunks an airing.

Swimming togs at dawn.

Goodnight, Euan.

Goodnight, Poppy.

Reluctant to let her go, he waited a few minutes to make sure she didn't send another message.

A light haze stretched over the sea, and the sun had yet to burn away the early morning clouds. But it was a mild morning.

Poppy felt exposed in her aquamarine and white polka dot swimsuit even though it flattered her figure. She kept a large towel draped around her shoulders while Euan slipped off his trousers to show that he was wearing a pair of swimming trunks. His long legs were lean and strong.

He cast his trousers, and the rolled up towel he'd brought, on the sand. Then he pulled off the light grey top he was wearing to reveal a leanly muscled torso and broad shoulders. His skin was smooth and bore the remnants of a summer working bare-chested in the sun.

Poppy hoped she wasn't staring and that he hadn't noticed the flustered look on her face. She'd felt her heart flutter a few times recently, admiring Euan with his clothes on. But now stripped down to a pair of trunks, his potent attraction was accentuated, along with his other assets. With this muscular man standing gazing at her, she was sure he could tell the effect his raw masculinity had on her.

'Last one in bakes the next cake,' he shouted and ran towards the sea.

Having no time to gather her senses, Poppy threw her towel off and raced after him.

Euan entered the water first and punched the air in triumph. 'A cherry cake would be nice.'

Poppy gasped as the cold water took her breath away. Either Euan was sucking up the cold, or was accustomed to swimming in all weathers.

His shoulders glistened with droplets of water, and he scooped up handfuls and washed it over his face and through his hair, sweeping it back and grinning at her.

'Cherry cake? Did you have that planned, knowing you'd cheat and run into the sea before I was ready?'

The broad shoulders shrugged. 'I'd settle for a Dundee cake if cherry's not your thing to bake.'

'I can and will bake a cherry cake.'

He smiled at her and she felt her heart ache looking at him standing there thigh deep in the sea. The water ran rivulets over his six-pack. Yes, he had one. She knew he would.

Euan was feeling the cold standing in the water. He pointed to a buoy further along the shore. 'Want to swim to the buoy and then back here?'

Poppy nodded, and without giving Euan time to get ready, she started swimming, getting a head start. She could hear him laughing as the water swept past her. It had been years since she'd gone swimming in the sea. Heated indoor pools were more her style, and even that was an activity she'd let drift as work ate up all her spare time.

Euan powered after her, catching up, but it wasn't an easy challenge to win. Poppy was fit, a strong swimmer and determined to challenge him. He admired her, and not only her attractive figure in the swimsuit, he loved that she challenged him in so many ways.

He swam along with her, smiling, and she smiled back at him, astounded that she was swimming in the sea, in the early autumn, with this handsome man. She hadn't known him long, but she felt comfortable with Euan.

'Turn here,' he shouted, diving under the water and emerging in the lead on the home straight.

'Oh, no you don't!' she shouted at him, putting on a spurt to beat him.

In the thrashing finish it was hard to tell the winner.

They both stood up at the same time, though she was inclined to think that Euan won. He thought the same about her. They agreed to call it a draw.

'I'll beat you next time,' Poppy said, walking out of the sea on to the sand where her towel was lying. She sat down on it and swept her hair back from her face.

Euan joined her. 'Next time?'

Poppy laughed.

The urge to lean over and kiss those smiling lips of hers was torturous to suppress, but he didn't dare compromise her.

'Do you think we'll have any energy left for a night of raucous dancing at the party?' he asked her, leaning back and grinning at her.

She tried and failed not to admire his lean torso. 'No, and we haven't even done our work yet.'

Euan sighed heavily and gazed out at the sea. 'We could abscond for the day.'

'Where would we go? What would we do?'

'I have no idea.' He shook his head in dismay. 'I'm not the absconding type.'

'Very well behaved.'

'I don't know about that,' he said, and then shook his wet hair in her direction.

'Stop that!'

They chided each other playfully and then raced towards the esplanade. Poppy was about to win, but Euan grabbed hold of her, lifted her up, swung her around and put her down.

'Behave yourself,' she scolded him playfully. 'People will think we're—'

'We're what?' He towered over her, and his handsome face smiled at her.

'That we're more than just friends.'

'Would that be so bad?'

She didn't have an immediate answer.

'Sorry, I'm just having fun with you.'

Poppy almost relented. Would it be so bad? No, not if he truly liked her. But there it was again, that doubt, worrying about another broken heart when she was so happy with her new life in the cottage. She needed time, that's what they both needed, and with the party night looming close, she wanted to concentrate on that, on enjoying an evening of ceilidh dancing without any awkwardness at the end of the night.

Euan seemed to read her well, and didn't push any further. 'Come on, I'll walk you back to the cottage, then I really have to tend the fields. A busy day.'

His attitude relieved the pressure and reset the easy friendship between them again.

'I'll drop by around seven,' he said when they reached the cottage garden. 'I could drive us down, but as it's only a couple of minutes walk—'

'I'd rather walk down. I'm enjoying being out in the evening air.'

'Unless it rains.'

'Agreed,' she said, and then waved him off. He'd put his clothes on, but his hair was still wet and glistened in the morning light as he walked away. She admired the handsome and sexy figure striding across the fields and looked forward to seeing him that evening.

The day flew by in a flurry of work, and then Poppy started to get herself ready for the party. She showered, dried her hair smooth and silky, applied her makeup and took the dress off the hanger. She'd made her decision.

'The blue one,' Euan said, arriving on time, carrying a bunch of roses and other flowers. 'You look beautiful, Poppy.'

Her senses were stirred by the tall, handsome kiltie standing in the living room.

He suited wearing the blue tartan kilt, and woollen socks with traditional dark shoes. His white Ghillie shirt laced up at the neck instead of having buttons, and was so sexy looking, emphasising his chest and broad shoulders. Tucked into the waist of his kilt, it suited his lean physique. The outfit was finished with a belt and buckle and a sporran.

'You look handsome,' she said.

He smiled and handed her the flowers.

'Thank you. I'll pop these in a vase and then we'll get going.' She'd set a vase up, anticipating that Euan would arrive with a bunch of flowers like he'd told her. She'd also kept a safety pin handy, then picked one of the white roses and pinned it to her handbag.

He smiled, pleased that she'd done this. 'Shall we go?'

They chatted about their respective days, and soon they heard the sound of laughter and music filtering out of the bar restaurant. The esplanade was busy with people heading to the party night.

Inside, the excitement was electric, and the atmosphere boosted Poppy's energy, causing her to smile.

Jock was the first to welcome them, and he couldn't wait to take them over to the bar where the framed embroidery was hanging up. 'Judy loves it!' he exclaimed. 'Thank you, Poppy.'

Euan didn't know what was going on, but when Poppy explained, he was happy that she'd done this for Jock and Judy.

'I promised Jock I'd keep it a secret so he could surprise Judy,' Poppy explained.

Judy waved over to Poppy and gave her the thumbs up. 'I love it,' she shouted over the lively music and chatter.

Poppy smiled and waved back.

'Let's go through to the function room,' said Euan. 'It'll get even busier in the bar and restaurant area, so we'll claim our spot near the dance floor.'

Nodding up at Euan, Poppy followed him through.

Minnie and Pearl were already seated at a table in the function room. Shawn was seated with them, along with another member of the quilting bee and her husband. They waved to each other, but there was no time to chat at that moment.

The atmosphere became even more charged with excitement as Jock announced that the ceilidh dancing was about to start. 'Take your partners for the first dance of the evening.'

Poppy recognised the dance from the music. She glanced at Euan. He'd no idea what the dance was, but as he didn't know one ceilidh dance from another, it didn't matter.

Poppy linked arms with Euan as they swirled around the dance floor. She tried to keep him right.

She attempted not to laugh as he kept sending them off in the wrong direction.

'Just keep going, Euan,' Poppy called to him over the sound of the lively music.

Euan made an effort to get it right, and some of the dance lessons he'd had previously from Jock kicked in. He remembered parts of the dance.

'You're a great dancer, Poppy,' said Euan.

She smiled at him and they danced on.

Three dances in and Euan was starting to pick up some of the steps from Poppy. The dances required him to partner with Minnie and Judy at times, and others during a reel, but he was always pleased when he was partnered again with Poppy. He could see the admiring looks at her from many of the locals, those that didn't know she was great at ceilidh dancing.

Her blue dress was perfect for the dancing, and she felt she'd made the right choice to wear it. Holding hands with Euan as they whirled around made her realise she'd also made the right choice to accompany him to the party.

While she sat out one of the dances, Euan came back with two refreshing drinks from the bar. She'd opted for lemonade and he joined her.

She sipped her cold drink and smiled around her. Minnie was up dancing with Shawn, and there were times when it seemed as if her feet barely touched the floor as his big, strong arms lifted her off it.

'Is that a new technique Minnie's got for the dancing?' Euan joked. 'Her feet are barely on the floor.'

Poppy joined in the joke. 'Yes, it's a special technique.'

'Oh, so you know it then?' Euan stood up and pulled Poppy into the dancing. 'Let's try it, shall we?'

Without giving Poppy a chance to object, Euan lifted her up and whirled her around.

She held on to him, giggling and shouting. 'No, Euan, no. Put me down.'

'I can't hear you above the music, Poppy,' he said cheekily.

This made her laugh even more, and caused her to give in to the merriment.

When the music paused, Euan led her back to their table to sip her lemonade.

'You're a rascal,' she said between sips.

'But you're having fun, eh?'

'I am, Euan.' She smiled at him and her heart squeezed seeing his handsome face gazing at her.

'Poppy!' Jock called to her, approaching with a purposeful swagger. 'I've had requests to demonstrate my party piece.' He named his favourite dance. 'It's supposed to be for two. Would you partner with me to give the folks a load of what this dance is like with real fancy footwork?'

Poppy glanced at Euan. He was nodding his encouragement, eager to see the impromptu performance.

'They won't think we're showing off?' she said hesitantly to Jock.

Jock frowned. 'Of course we're showing off. Come on, lass, let's give them a show for their money.'

Poppy let Jock lead her on to the dance floor.

Jock announced in a booming voice, 'I've had requests to dance my party piece, and we've a top notch wee dancer here tonight, so Poppy's going to accompany me.'

The crowd cheered Poppy.

'Take it away, Judy,' Jock shouted.

Judy turned up the music. Everyone gathered round in cheerful anticipation.

Jock and Poppy bowed and curtsied, as they'd done the last time she'd danced with him.

'Pull out all the stops, Poppy,' Jock encouraged her.

She nodded and then they were off, fancy footwork taking them flying across the floor, circling the room, and then Poppy stood clapping while Jock did his part of the display.

Euan cheered and whistled when it was Poppy's turn. She outdid herself with the tricky footwork, her Highland dance skills coming in to play. The skirt of her dress emphasised her spinning, almost balletic when she did her fast spins with her arms arched high.

If there was a moment when Euan realised that he'd fallen in love with Poppy, it was then, watching her dancing. If she gave him a chance, he knew his love would deepen even more.

A men only dance followed Jock and Poppy's performance. Now it was time for the ladies to sit and watch the kilted men do a reel.

Euan gave a fair go at keeping in time, as did other recent learners including Shawn. By now Gordon had turned up, having closed the tea shop, and joined in.

Poppy, Minnie, Pearl and Judy stood together.

'They're a handsome lot, aren't they?' Judy commented, always pleased that her Jock was responsible for the ceilidh nights and keeping everyone right.

'Yes, they are,' Minnie and the other ladies agreed.

Poppy watched Euan and remembered what he'd said earlier... Would it be so bad to be more than friends? Would it? Love and romance were always a risk.

'Get ready to avert your eyes, ladies,' Judy said to them. 'The whirly spins are coming up.'

Minnie and Pearl knew what she meant, but Poppy frowned.

'The bits where the men's kilts can go flying up to reveal...well...' Judy winked.

'Their bare bahookies and bells,' Pearl elaborated.

Poppy laughed, thinking they might be exaggerating, but no...she saw what they meant as the swirl of their kilts gave a hint that they'd all gone commando.

'I wish Shawn would lengthen his pleats,' said Minnie.

'It's not the length of his pleats that people are cheering,' Judy said, grinning at her.

The ladies giggled as the music finally slowed down and the reel was finished.

Loud applause, whistles and clapping filled the function room.

Before the next dance, Poppy saw Shawn approach Jock at the music system, and whisper something. Jock nodded, and turned the music down to make an announcement.

Euan and Gordon were now standing with Poppy and the ladies.

'Can I have your attention for a wee moment, folks,' Jock began. 'Shawn would like to say something.' He handed the microphone to Shawn.

'I won't take up your evening,' Shawn began. 'But I'd like to ask Minnie to step up here for a moment.'

Everyone looked at Minnie. She'd no idea what Shawn was doing. The ladies quickly urged her to step up. Minnie put down her glass of sherry lemonade with a cherry in it, and walked over to Shawn.

He smiled at her and got down on one knee.

The crowd erupted, then Jock indicated for them to hush.

'I was wondering...' Shawn dug into his sporran and pulled out a jewellery box. 'Would you'd like to marry me, Minnie?'

Minnie gasped.

'You don't have to feel pressured into marrying me right away. I don't want to rush you. But I'm hoping you'll want to become engaged, for as long as you want, no pressure, and make us an official couple.'

Shawn opened the box to reveal a beautiful diamond ring.

Minnie blinked. 'You've got a big sparkler!'

'And a ring for you, Minnie,' he said, causing laughter to erupt.

Euan glanced at Poppy and smiled.

'Give me your hand, Minnie,' said Shawn.

Minnie giggled and held out her hand and Shawn slipped the ring on her finger.

Everyone cheered.

Jock played the music and the dancing continued, with Minnie and Shawn taking to the floor.

'I'm so happy for them,' Poppy said to Euan.

At that moment, Gordon came running over to Euan. 'Judy's struggling in the kitchen. They're short–staffed and extra busy. Want to come and give me a hand to catch up on the orders?'

Euan glanced at Poppy.

'Go ahead, I'm fine. I'll relax for a wee bit.'

Euan and Gordon hurried through to the kitchen.

Judy was relieved to see them.

They scrubbed up and put aprons on.

Euan began ladling up the Scotch broth. It felt strange wearing an apron with his kilt.

'It's quite freeing wearing a kilt in the kitchen,' said Gordon, serving up the stovies.

'A new outfit to consider, Gordon,' said Euan. 'And a nice surprise for Eila when she gets home from Edinburgh.'

'I'm planning a better surprise than that — a romantic night, hearts, flowers, balloons and presenting her with a ring.'

'You should still wear your kilt,' Judy advised. 'Make it extra special.'

Gordon nodded. 'I'll do that.'

Through in the function room, a good looking farmer approached Poppy. 'I know you're with Euan, but while he's busy, would you care to dance with me?'

Poppy nodded and accompanied him in the dancing.

When Euan came back to the dancing, he felt a stab of jealousy through his heart when he saw Poppy enjoying herself with the farmer. One of the local charmers. He hated feeling like this, but couldn't help himself. Another indication of the strength of his feelings for Poppy.

'It's you she likes,' Jock whispered to him. 'Cut–in,' he urged Euan.

'I don't want her to think I'm the jealous type,' said Euan.

'We're all the jealous type when it comes to our ladies, now get over there and fight for her,' Jock told him. 'You're always missing out by dragging your heels.'

Euan nodded to Jock and then wound his way through the dancing until he was next to Poppy and the farmer. 'My turn, I think.'

The look that Euan gave him, although not aggressive, was clear. This was his lady.

The farmer smiled at Poppy and stepped away.

Euan danced with Poppy and she was glad that he'd come back.

As the dance finished, he led her off the floor.

'Everything okay now in the kitchen?' she said, smiling at him.

Her smile reassured him that Jock's advice had been right.

'Yes, Judy just got a bit too busy, but the backlog is cleared now.'

'You've become quite the chef.'

He shook his head. 'I ladled the soup and cut the bread.'

Minnie came hurrying over to Poppy. 'Want to make a wish?' she offered, slipping her diamond engagement ring off.

'It's a beautiful ring, Minnie,' said Poppy.

'It's a dazzler!' Minnie then encouraged Poppy to put it on. 'Turn it around three times and make a wish.'

Poppy put the ring on, turned it three times, closed her eyes and made a wish.

'I hope it comes true,' said Minnie.

Poppy handed the ring back to Minnie. 'I've had two wishes lately.'

Minnie eyed her with Euan. 'Maybe one has come true already.' Smiling, she hurried away to let Pearl have a wish on her ring.

'Do you think it has?' Euan asked Poppy.

She shrugged. 'I don't know. Maybe a little bit.'

Euan remembered what Jock had said about dragging his heels. He always missed out on his chances when it came to romance. He decided to risk everything and put his arms gently around her, pulling her close to him, gazing down at her.

Poppy didn't resist.

'I was thinking about what you said earlier down the shore,' she said softly.

He knew what she meant. He pulled her closer. 'Would it be so bad to be more than friends?' he asked her.

This time her answer came from the heart. The truth, even though it bore a risk. 'No, I don't think it would be bad at all.'

'Neither do I,' he murmured.

Amid all the merriment circling around them, Poppy and Euan only had eyes for each other.

'Take a chance on me, Poppy. I won't ever let you down, or break your heart. I promise you.'

She smiled up at him and nodded, her heart fluttering, seeing a future with Euan, beginning tonight, taking things slowly but aiming for the type of happiness that Jock and Judy, Gordon and Eila and Minnie and Shawn had.

'Would you like to dance with me?' He offered her his hand.

Poppy accepted his hand without any further hesitation.

As they danced and enjoyed themselves with their friends, Poppy took a moment to whisper to Euan.

'Just to let you know,' Poppy said, smiling up at him. 'Wishes do come true.'

Euan smiled back at her, pulled her close and kissed her. They kissed lovingly, longingly and then continued to dance as a couple.

End

Bee Embroidery Pattern

A bee embroidery pattern designed by the author, De-ann Black, is included here. It is pictured on the back cover of the book.

The pattern is printed to scale on page 103 with instructions on page 105.

You also can download a printable version of the pattern from the book's accompanying website:
www.De-annBlack.com/BeePattern

Bee Embroidery Pattern

Note:
You will need to trace the pattern on to fabric.
De-ann's method is included in a video on the book's website.
De-annBlack.com/BeePattern

Bee Embroidery Pattern

Note:
You will need to trace the pattern on to fabric.
De-ann's method is included in a video on the book's website.
De-annBlack.com/BeePattern

Use single strands of stranded cotton thread.
The fabric used was cotton.
Hoop size: 6 or 7 inches.

Arms & legs - back stitch - black.
Antennae - back stitch - black.
Head - long & short stitch - black.
Eyes - satin stitch - grey.

Wings - outline - stem stitch - beige.
Wings - veins - stem stitch - grey.

Long & short stitch - black.
Add straight stitches - brown.

Long & short stitch - amber yellow.

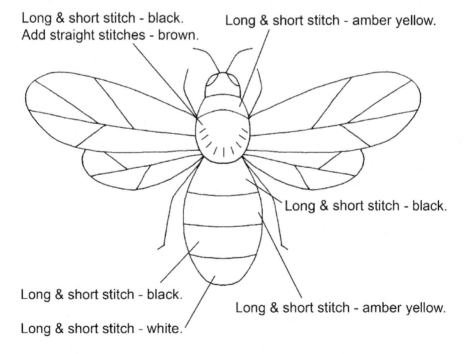

Long & short stitch - black.

Long & short stitch - black.

Long & short stitch - amber yellow.

Long & short stitch - white.

About the Author:

De-ann Black is a bestselling author, scriptwriter and former newspaper journalist. She has over 80 books published. Romance, crime thrillers, espionage novels, action adventure. And children's books (non-fiction rocket science books and children's fiction). She became an Amazon All-Star author in 2014 and 2015.

She previously worked as a full-time newspaper journalist for several years. She had her own weekly columns in the press. This included being a motoring correspondent where she got to test drive cars every week for the press for three years.

Before being asked to work for the press, De-ann worked in magazine editorial writing everything from fashion features to social news. She was the marketing editor of a glossy magazine. She is also a professional artist and illustrator. Fabric design, dressmaking, sewing, knitting and fashion are part of her work.

Additionally, De-ann has always been interested in fitness, and was a fitness and bodybuilding champion, 100 metre runner and mountaineer. As a former N.A.B.B.A. Miss Scotland, she had a weekly fitness show on the radio that ran for over three years.

De-ann trained in Shukokai karate, boxing, kickboxing, Dayan Qigong and Jiu Jitsu. She is currently based in Scotland.
Her colouring books and embroidery design books are available in paperback. These include Floral Nature Embroidery Designs and Scottish Garden Embroidery Designs.

Also by De-ann Black (Romance, Action/Thrillers & Children's books). See her Amazon Author page or website for further details about her books, screenplays, illustrations, art and fabric designs. www.De-annBlack.com

Romance books:

Cottages, Cakes & Crafts series:
1. The Flower Hunter's Cottage
2. The Sewing Bee by the Sea
3. The Beemaster's Cottage
4. The Chocolatier's Cottage
5. The Bookshop by the Seaside
6. The Dressmaker's Cottage

Sewing, Crafts & Quilting series:
1. The Sewing Bee
2. The Sewing Shop

Quilting Bee & Tea Shop series:
1. The Quilting Bee
2. The Tea Shop by the Sea
3. Embroidery Cottage

Heather Park: Regency Romance

Snow Bells Haven series:
1. Snow Bells Christmas
2. Snow Bells Wedding

Summer Sewing Bee
Christmas Cake Chateau

Sewing, Knitting & Baking series:
1. The Tea Shop
2. The Sewing Bee & Afternoon Tea
3. The Christmas Knitting Bee
4. Champagne Chic Lemonade Money
5. The Vintage Sewing & Knitting Bee

The Tea Shop & Tearoom series:
1. The Christmas Tea Shop & Bakery
2. The Christmas Chocolatier
3. The Chocolate Cake Shop in New York at Christmas
4. The Bakery by the Seaside
5. Shed in the City

Tea Dress Shop series:
1. The Tea Dress Shop At Christmas
2. The Fairytale Tea Dress Shop In Edinburgh
3. The Vintage Tea Dress Shop In Summer

Christmas Romance series:
1. Christmas Romance in Paris
2. Christmas Romance in Scotland

Romance, Humour, Mischief series:
1. Oops! I'm the Paparazzi
2. Oops! I'm A Hollywood Agent
3. Oops! I'm A Secret Agent
4. Oops! I'm Up To Mischief

The Bitch-Proof Suit series:
1. The Bitch-Proof Suit
2. The Bitch-Proof Romance
3. The Bitch-Proof Bride

The Cure For Love
Dublin Girl
Why Are All The Good Guys Total Monsters?
I'm Holding Out For A Vampire Boyfriend

Action/Thriller books:
Love Him Forever
Someone Worse
Electric Shadows
The Strife Of Riley
Shadows Of Murder
Cast a Dark Shadow

Colouring books:
Flower Nature
Summer Garden
Spring Garden
Autumn Garden
Sea Dream
Festive Christmas
Christmas Garden
Christmas Theme
Flower Bee
Wild Garden
Faerie Garden Spring
Flower Hunter
Stargazer Space
Bee Garden
Scottish Garden Seasons

Embroidery Design books:
Floral Garden Embroidery Patterns
Floral Spring Embroidery Patterns
Christmas & Winter Embroidery Patterns
Floral Nature Embroidery Designs
Scottish Garden Embroidery Designs

Printed in Great Britain
by Amazon

19942415R00068